EVERYTHING HE WANTS

LISA HUGHEY

Salty Kisses Press, LLC

Everything He Wants

Billionaire Breakfast Club: #2
By
Lisa Hughey

Copyright February 2018

Salty Kisses Press, LLC

Lisa Hughey

Ebook ISBN: 978-0-9991951-2-3

Amazon Print ISBN: 978-0-9991951-4-7

Ingram ISBN: 978-1-950359-26-4

Audio ISBN: 978-1-950359-23-3

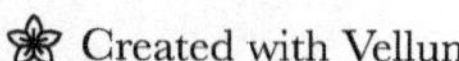 Created with Vellum

Prologue

D'ANDRE SMITH, STAR RUNNING BACK FOR HIS SEVENTH grade Midget team, loped toward the locker room. He needed to get home and make his mother dinner. She'd worked an extra shift this week to pay for his new gear.

"Smith," his coach barked.

D'Andre jerked to a stop. "Yes, Coach?"

"Let's go back out to the field and repeat your footwork drills."

"I need to do my homework, sir."

"I'll get someone to take care of that for you."

"But—"

"Smith." Coach clapped his hand on D'Andre's shoulder. "That ain't your future, son."

His stomach growled.

"Your mama working tonight?"

D'Andre nodded, holding in the words he wanted to shout. He needed to do his homework. Or at least try. He didn't understand his books. When he listened he was fine. And once he heard something, he never forgot. He understood everything, but when he tried to make sense of the words on the page, everything got jumbled in his head and he just kept getting further and further behind.

"Let's put in a couple more hours and I'll get you some Mickey D's." Coach bent his head toward D'Andre. "There's a scout from up north coming next week. We've got to be ready. This could be big. Really big."

"But I need to keep up my grades, sir." He needed to figure out what the heck the letters on the page meant. He could sound out some words, but he couldn't do that in class. If he did, people would make fun of him. He remembered what happened last year when he'd misread a simple poem.

Miss Higgins had finally given him a recording so he could memorize the words. It was their secret that he couldn't read them.

But that grinding frustration drilled deep in his belly, digging into his gut. His stomach churned and his heart shriveled.

"Listen, son. Football's your future." Coach gave him a hard pat on his head. "Don't worry none about schooling. Your coaches will take care of you."

And they did.

Chapter One

Elise Putnam needed a life.

She slung her leather briefcase over her shoulder, and headed down the grand staircase of her family mansion. She was stagnating, turning to dust like an old relic consigned to the attic, and she was only twenty-four.

Her footsteps were soft on the Persian-carpeted stairs, masking her approach to her regularly scheduled, awkward morning conversation with her father. At the base of the stairs, she paused, forced a placid expression on her face, and dropped her briefcase on the antique chair that flanked the staircase. She squared her shoulders and girded for the next half hour.

Keith Putnam sat at the head of the massive dining room table, readers perched on his nose. He scanned *The Wall Street Journal* in his right hand, while to his left a state-of-the-art tablet showed running stock exchange numbers. An empty Wedgewood china plate, sterling silver flatware, and a delicate coffee cup were the remnants of his daily breakfast of scrambled eggs and wheat toast with precisely one cup of high octane java. He perused her critically, his gaze skimming over her business attire, and his lips tightened in displeasure. The small censure evaporated her earlier resolve.

Elise ignored that instinctive ping of hurt, refusing to let him win this round. Using the slotted serving spoon, she placed a small amount of scrambled eggs and half slice of bacon on her plate. Franny, their house maid, served a cup of coffee at the other end of the table, formerly her mother's spot. She shot Elise a sympathetic smile and left the room immediately.

"What's on your agenda for today?" her father asked.

Elise tightened her shoulders, lifted her chin, and said softly, "I'm going in to the office." Like she did every day since her father had gotten her this job at *Yankee Sports Magazine*. Maybe today she'd be given more responsibility than just copyediting someone else's work. Maybe today she could move into a more active role in the research and crafting of their monthly articles.

"Pfft." Her father set down his paper with the snap. "When are you going to stop playing at reporter and get down to what you were meant to do?"

Elise didn't answer. Didn't want to answer.

Her father wasn't done. "Your purpose in life is to breed. It's time to begin working on the new generation of Putnams."

And now her morning was officially ruined. According to her father, her only value lay in her looks and her ability to pass on his genes. She set her fork on the delicate china plate, her appetite gone. She folded her hands in front of her, noting with a sense of detachment that her French manicure was perfect. "I wish to have a career. And I like working at *Yankee Sports*."

She could relate to athletes. Their drive, their push for physical excellence, their goal setting and achievement.

"Your wishes don't matter." The great Keith Putnam had spoken.

Her earlier excitement curdled in her stomach, and disappointment rose in a tide of bile. She glanced away from her father, focused on the muted wallpaper and thick velvet draperies, the mullioned windows and arched doorways, before settling on the swinging door that led to the servant's hallways and quarters. The house's traditional style hadn't changed for a hundred years. Kind of like her father's attitude.

She didn't want this life. But she had to prove to everyone that she could survive on her own. She didn't have access to her trust fund until she turned twenty-seven. Three long years from now.

"My secretary has emailed a list of suitable candidates." Keith adjusted the cuff on his five-thousand-dollar Anderson & Sheppard bespoke suit and folded his paper. "I expect you to begin the process of choosing a husband."

She didn't want a husband. She didn't want to breed. She wanted a *life*.

"I have an engagement this evening, but I expect you to read the list and get back to me with your choices ranked by end of day."

There would be no arguing with him.

The only way to stop the procreation train was to start earning enough money so she could escape the rigid and dismissive iron-fisted control of her father.

"Your period of mourning is over." Her father stood, staring at her as if his gaze could incinerate her feelings and leave her as an unemotional robot who churned out his mini-heirs.

It didn't matter what she wanted, and that was the worst of all.

"While your mother's death was tragic, it's time to get over it."

After caring for her terminally ill mother, after putting her life on hold for years, now when she was ready to experience everything, what she wanted didn't matter to him.

For over two years, she had been the one to stay with her mother as she declined, her body and soul ravaged from the effects of cancer. Not that they couldn't afford extra help. A live-in nurse had also been on call. But Elise's duty was to her parents (as her father saw it) and that was that. She'd been trapped here since she graduated from college.

"There's a good girl." Her father smiled, and she swore if she'd been closer he would've patted her on the head like a faithful dog.

After years of verbal criticism, his castigation bordered on abuse, although in his eyes he would never be guilty of anything so crass. He was merely head of the household exerting his will on his offspring.

But one constant settled in her heart: his dismissals hurt.

"You will do what you are told."

Elise left the dining room after a short goodbye without acknowledging his edict. She had no intention of picking out a husband from a catalog like he was her favorite of the latest Bergdorf offerings.

Her father just assumed she would fall in line with what he wanted. It never occurred to him that she would disobey his wishes. She never had before. But what he wanted wasn't temporary.

While she'd tended to her mother, she'd read romance

novels. She wanted a grand passion, not some clinical union based strictly on money and genetics. She wanted love. Romance. And she had no intention of settling for anything less.

Her father was in for a rude awakening. She was just too stubborn to give in. She'd talk to her boss, press him for more opportunities to show to the world and especially her father, that she had what it took to be a successful reporter.

Right now, she didn't make enough to support herself on her miniscule salary. Her friends from prep school were all living in New York or Boston with high-powered jobs in finance and real estate, and she had lost touch with her college friends. Sure, she kept up on Facebook but they had these amazing interesting lives and everyone had left her behind. In her mind, she didn't have anything to add, and she'd languished for the past few years, almost a recluse in her family home. But no more.

She had to get out and start to live her life on her terms. She had to.

⁂

ONE OF THE feature reporters tilted his head over their shared wall of the cubicles. "Elise, boss wants to see you."

"Me?" She had just set down her briefcase on the extra chair jammed into her six-by-six space. Her heart picked up a little. She hated to get her hopes up but maybe she'd finally get an exciting assignment.

Maybe this would be her opportunity to get out of the untenable position her father put her in.

"Yeah. But just a warning, he is in a *mood*."

With that her hopes plummeted. "Going now."

She rubbed her damp palms down her pinstriped pants and breathed deep. Closing her eyes, she settled her thoughts, squared her shoulders, and strode confidently to his office.

"Elise." Her boss's voice slithered over her name. Dick Johnson called everyone else in the office by their last name except her. His smile was tight, not his usual smarmy with a touch of sleaze. "Come in."

"You wanted to see me, sir?"

He didn't look happy. And Elise wondered if maybe she was getting fired.

"You know Jason Hollingsworth?"

Inside she was having a mini-freakout. She couldn't get fired. She needed this job.

"The fourth?" he clarified.

"Jay?" She finally tracked back into the conversation but she was definitely confused. Why in the world would he be asking her about Jay Hollingsworth? "Um, yes. We went to prep school together."

He jerked his chin up. "He's requested you for a story."

She still didn't have any idea why Jay would request her or what a venture capitalist would have to do with a sports magazine but she kept her mouth shut and waited.

Dick Johnson skipped his gaze around his office, stopping on the various accolades and photos with famous athletes hanging on the wall before he turned back to her.

"What do you know about D'Andre Smith?"

"Ultra-famous wide receiver, retired early because of concussions or he would have likely become one of the best receivers in football history. Intensely private. Never gives interviews."

He slapped a folder on his desk. "Apparently he's willing to give an interview, but only to you."

D'Andre Smith? And he would only speak to *her*? She couldn't process what her boss was saying. D'Andre Smith was the ungettable get. And he wanted her?

A fierce pride rose inside her.

"I tried to convince Hollingsworth that Smith should go with someone with more experience, someone who could actually pull off this interview. But he refused to consider anyone else."

With that, her confidence blew out like a hiss of air. Elise was used to hiding her emotions, so she lifted her gaze to her boss, the Dick. "When?" She needed serious prep time for this interview. This was literally the opportunity of the decade.

She needed to read everything she could get her hands on and she needed to watch film and she had to find the angle for the story. Her mind was racing with all the things she needed to do to prepare for writing the profile of her career.

Dick twisted his wrist. "You've got two and a half hours."

What?!

"But—"

"We need to come up with a news peg." Dick said, "You know what that is?"

Elise's temper rose. "Of course, sir." She may not have much, okay, *any* real world experience but she'd worked for her university paper and gotten her degree in journalism.

"Find an angle to make this newsworthy." He shoved the folder at her. "I've got final approval over every word in the article. And see if you can convince Smith to agree to a photo shoot."

"Yes, sir."

"And Putnam?"

"Sir?"

"Don't fuck this up."

Or you're fired was implied.

Chapter Two

D'Andre Smith had it all.

Fame. Money. Women. On the outside, his life looked fucking perfect.

And if it wasn't, no way would he admit it to anyone. He flipped back the cuff on his hand-tailored Italian dress shirt, the cotton softer than the toilet paper he'd used as a kid, and checked the time on his Cartier Calibre watch. The reporter (how had he let himself get roped into that?) wasn't late. He was early.

He had a few minutes to go over his game plan for dealing with this interview. He hated the press. He kept his private life *private*. His pal Jay—Jason Hollingsworth IV for the society crowd—had insisted that D needed to start playing the media game to build buzz for the launch of his new company and its extremely important product, the concussion detection helmet.

Nonetheless, he'd still been tempted to bail on this interview. But Peter Nguyen, another friend from his sounding board, the BBC—Billionaire Breakfast Club—had agreed with Jay. So here he was waiting for a reporter, some prep school friend of Jay's, which was pretty much the only way he would agree to speak with the press. And when his momma found out, there was gonna be hell to pay.

Momma hated reporters. *Hated.* He wasn't fond of them either but after a particularly rough interview and story printed about her, Mary Smith had made him promise not to talk to them. He hadn't yet told her that he was going to have to break her cardinal rule.

The biggest problem with reporters was they always wanted to stick their nose in shit that was none of their business. As a result, he'd learned to dazzle and deflect like a pro.

He smiled at the hostess at Parker's Restaurant as she led him to his regular table in the formal dining room of the Omni Parker House Hotel in downtown Boston. His mother's favorite place. After the interview, he needed to meet with the catering director about his mother's fiftieth birthday party. It was going to be a surprise. And he wanted everything to be perfect.

Mary Smith deserved a banging party and he was going to make sure she got one.

Within a few seconds, the waiter placed sparkling water in front of him. "Your usual, Mr. Smith."

"Thanks, José."

"My pleasure, sir."

D pulled out his phone and clumsily texted his momma a good morning.

Predictably, his phone rang. "Hi, Momma."

"You know I don't like that texting. Why don't anyone just pick up a phone and call anymore?"

D'Andre sighed. "I didn't want to bother you."

"Talkin' to my baby boy is never a bother." She sniffed. He was six four and two hundred seventy pounds, down thirty from his NFL career days, but to his mother he was still her baby.

"Thanks, Momma." His voice softened and his mouth curved. "Everything okay there?" He'd bought her the house in Brookline with his signing bonus ten years ago.

"The newfangled dishwasher is running rough."

"I'll get a repairman out there first thing."

"Thanks, baby."

"Anything for you," D'Andre said softly. His mother had sacrificed her best years to support him. Now it was his turn. "What's on your agenda for today?"

His mother kinda sounded like she was huffing and puffing. "Meeting some girls from church for an early birthday lunch."

A rustling behind him caught his ear and D turned around to see a stunning woman approaching his table.

Once during his rookie year in the NFL, he'd taken a hit so hard he'd been flat out on his back, the turf prickling his calves, breath clawing to escape his chest. The sky had swirled above him, a bright brilliant blue while he tried to remember who, and where, he was.

With one glance at this woman's dazzling ice blue eyes, his heart thunked in his chest and his head swirled, as if he'd taken a similar hit. That sensation of being flat out gobsmacked pummeled him just like that monster tackle from a three-hundred-fifty pound linebacker. He shook his head, trying to clear the sensation of having his bell rung.

Fuck him.

She wore a mannish navy suit with matching pointy flats. Not the least bit sexy. And yet he wanted to pull her into his embrace and hold on tight. A waterfall of straight platinum hair framed a stunning face of classic bone structure, bright blue eyes and a wide, unsmiling mouth.

"Mr. Smith." Not a question. Slightly haughty, frosty, ice princess.

He realized he'd been far too silent and his mother had been chattering away on the other end of the line.

"Well then, have a good lunch." He managed to finish his call without babbling like an idiot. He blindly pressed the end button. He guessed this was the reporter. She certainly didn't dress like a groupie.

That untouchable queen to peasant thing was really doing it for him. He'd never had this kind of physical reaction to a woman in his life. But he had to ignore it. Because her profession killed any possibility of engaging beyond this interview. Reporters were off-limits. For so, *so* many reasons.

So instead of asking her on a date, preferably one that started right here and ended upstairs in the Harvey Parker suite with both of them naked, he was going to ignore this insane attraction and do what he always did.

Flirt, distract, deflect, and get rid of her fast after he got his message across. He'd be out of here in thirty. He'd ignore his visceral reaction and get it done.

❦

THIS WAS IT. Her big assignment. She needed this win.

D'Andre Smith rose to his feet gracefully.

The guy was huge. Big for a receiver, he stood a good four or five inches over her six foot frame.

Her breath caught. He was big. Black. Physically impressive.

He wore a custom-tailored navy suit with a white cotton dress shirt. Hair in a low-fade cut with medium-length twists, and a smooth sexy shave that showcased his rich ebony skin and accented his mouth.

And the libido that had lain dormant for two years roared to life at his proximity. Her hormones sparked and flared like firecrackers on the Fourth. Arousal sang in her body and danced in her blood.

But this was not the time, and he was definitely not the man, to break her sex fast with. She had a lot to prove, and getting involved with D'Andre Smith, her interview subject, would kill her career launch faster than an unverified source and false information.

She was not going to prove her father right. She had more value than being her future husband's arm candy and the vessel for the next generation of Putnams.

"Mr. Smith." She shoved out her hand, determined to put them on the proper footing.

His large hand engulfed hers, making her feel almost dainty. Her girl parts shivered with appreciation for his fit body and impressive muscles.

"Call me D." His deep voice rumbled through her, setting off mini-detonations in her midsection. Her brain should be screaming a warning at her: *Danger ahead*.

"Nice to meet you." Oh hell no, that was not her voice, all sexed up and husky. She blanked her expression, channeling the calm she used when her father spoke down to her, and stood her ground, forcing herself not to take a strategic step back from all that testosterone. *Show no fear.* He was not going to intimidate her. If she gave ground, he'd never respect her. And if he didn't respect her, the tough questions would stay unanswered.

He was still holding her hand, which felt wonderful wrapped around hers.

"Likewise." That low smooth murmur fluttered through

her system, pollinating each erogenous zone, bringing it to stunning, completely inappropriate life. "Have a seat."

She wanted to drop into a puddle of unexpected lust. Elise breathed deep and lowered into the chair across from one the NFL's most famous wide receivers. He hadn't been in the game all that long, but while he'd played he'd made an impression on the public. He had retired after a third concussion and started his own company.

D'Andre Smith was known for his generosity, charm, and serial dating. He supported the community and donated lots of time to various causes. But for all his fame, D'Andre Smith was a very private guy. Her job was to get the goods on the famous ex-athlete, now business magnate.

Based on Dick Johnson's comments this morning, he didn't think she had a chance to get anything from this interview. Hell, as she was walking out the door, he'd actually suggested she should have sex with D'Andre to get information. He absolutely expected her to fail.

But Elise needed this job, needed to support herself.

To do that, she had to start getting creative.

D'Andre Smith was notorious for not giving interviews. Ever. Post-game sound bites were the most he'd ever given the press when he'd been a player, so of course that only whet the public's appetite for more.

His reluctance to speak was as legendary as his career stats and his noted reputation as a bit of a player. But he'd agreed to this interview, and Jay had insisted on her.

She wasn't naïve enough to think choosing her was because of her journalistic skill. She'd guess it was strategic. They probably thought she'd be easily charmed and distracted by his fame.

She wasn't about to let that happen.

She'd watched enough tape of him in various settings to

know that he used his innate charm to distract reporters and fans alike, garnering him impunity from criticism. In fact, he was beloved by everyone. After her research all she really knew was that he loved his mother.

No whiff of scandal or inappropriate behavior from football's golden boy. But no one could possibly be as squeaky clean as he came across.

She just needed to find out his secret. What no one else had discovered about him. That would be her angle for the story. She'd have to forgo the instinctive need to cringe over invasion of privacy and compassion. He was in the public eye, held to a different standard than mere mortals. She needed to find the hook that would set this interview apart.

Occasionally there was something about his friends. He hung out with a very successful crowd. Oddly no one else was a professional athlete. They ran the gamut. From wealthy socialites Tracy Thayer—who Elise knew peripherally from the yacht club—social media mogul, and her pal, Jay who had started his own venture capitalist firm after dropping out of college…to an eclectic mix of self-made entrepreneurs. Courtney Lee, a relatively famous gamer girl turned potential politician, who was running for office in 2018. Diego Ramos, son of immigrants, who grew up in Dot and started his own high-end auto parts empire. Duke Kalani, who'd burst onto the natural foods scene and quickly made a name for himself. And finally Peter Nguyen, a famous tech guru who'd recently had his company valued at over one billion dollars. Success was all they had in common as far she could tell. Some of them had gone to Ivy League schools but they hadn't all attended the same school. Elise had jotted notes about the various friends, determined to ask how he'd managed to join such a diverse group of people.

She flipped open her notebook, took out a pen, then held up her phone. "Do you mind if I also record our conversation? I like to go back and listen to the audio after I mock up my story."

He stared at her phone for an inordinate amount of time, then grudgingly nodded. "I'm partial to audio as well."

Her instincts started humming at his small wiggle of hesitation. "Thanks."

"For the record, this is an interview between D'Andre Smith, former NFL wide receiver, and Elise Putnam, writer for *Yankee Sports*." She smiled at him trying to put him at ease. "Thanks for agreeing to meet with me, Mr. Smith."

"D."

"Excuse me?"

"Call me, D." He smiled, his lips curved and his teeth gleamed brightly white against his dark skin. That smile warmed her from the inside out, the glow spreading through her like butter melting on a hot Parker House roll. "Before we start, let me have my friend José get you a drink."

Suspicion crowded out that arousal. Was he trying to get her drunk? "No alcohol, thank you."

"You can have whatever you want." Was she imagining that suggestive tone? Smith smiled at her, but his smile seemed vacant, practiced. And she literally saw him slip into some sort of role as he treated her more like a first date than a reporter who was a threat.

He'd written her off before they even started.

"Water is fine. Why don't we get started," she said, trying to firmly place them back into the realm of interviewer and interviewee.

For a moment that slick mask slipped. "I would never disappoint a fan."

But she wasn't just a fan.

"Especially one as pretty as you."

Did he really just try to reduce her to a pretty face?

She fought the urge to bristle. Getting defensive wouldn't help this interview go anywhere. She'd come up with some hard-hitting questions for everyone's favorite retired Patriot. But if she dove in with what she really wanted to know, she had a feeling, D'Andre Smith would finesse her right out the door.

Elise eased back in her chair, making her posture as nonthreatening as possible. "I have been a fan since your college days." Which was true.

He'd only played one year in college before entering the draft and gone in the third round. And even though many rookies didn't live up to their hype, D'Andre Smith had exceeded it.

"Go Tar Heels." His presence loomed across from her filling the silence, expanding in the void, and surrounding her with his particular brand of hotness. Why had no one ever mentioned how much his sexuality dominated a room?

She wanted to preen like a peacock, and fluff her feathers so he'd edge closer. She focused on her questions so she wouldn't reveal that he affected her on a physical level, protecting her inner soft core from ridicule. Typically the best way to start was with open-ended questions, to get the subject relaxed and then home in on more controversial topics.

Elbows on the arms of the chair, D clasped his hands together, steepling his fingers in front of his mouth. Could be a classic gesture to indicate he was about to lie. But her gaze went to his very large hands. And she had to wonder if he was big all over. God, she hadn't had a date in forever. She hadn't had a man between her thighs and powering into her since what felt like the Stone Age. And the completely inappropriate yet shockingly detailed image of him doing both stole her breath.

"You want to touch it?"

"Excuse me?" Elise reared back. Jeez, she could feel the violent flush spreading over her face.

"My ring."

"Oh. *Oh!*" Oh God, hopefully he hadn't figured out where her mind had gone.

He winked at her and held out his hand.

Shit. He knew exactly where she'd gone. And he'd led her right there. Mr. Super Bowl football player who never talked to the press was trying to fluster her so she wouldn't ask the tough questions. And suddenly she was pissed. Tired of men reducing her to a pretty face or an object to be owned and displayed. Screw him.

"I'd love to," she purred, pouring every ounce of sexy she could into her voice.

He blinked, his curled onyx lashes opening wider, showing his surprise and highlighting his hickory eyes.

That satisfied smirk disappeared and a heated sensual awareness shimmered in the air between them. She wasn't about to let some overgrown jock with a sense of superiority put one over on her. She was getting this interview. It was going to be the interview of the century and nothing was going to stop her. Not even Mr. Hotter than Hell, Panty-Dropping, Muscle-Bound Ex-Football Player.

You want to play? Game on.

Chapter Three

concussion injuries? Especially since you were cleared to play under dubious circumstances?"

D remembered his last run with the ball, the exhilaration, the dump of adrenaline, the sheer joy when he crossed into the end zone. And then that heart-stopping knowledge, that if the biggest, meanest cornerback in the NFL hadn't tripped, D would have been seriously injured. The hard-hitting beast had missed him by inches, and if he'd connected, D's brain would have been dangerously banged around when he wasn't near one hundred percent— that realization had been a huge wake-up call.

"I met the clearance protocols," he replied quietly. Disappointment, then speculation flashed in her eyes.

And shit. He might have seriously miscalculated.

But it was rare that he couldn't charm the questions right out of the head of the opposite sex. And he knew with a surety reserved for a perfect reverse handoff when he could score.

If you'd asked him five seconds ago, he'd have been assured of an additional six on the scoreboard.

But the affability and sex appeal that usually served him slid away when her smile flipped from flustered prey to predatory in an instant. He'd severely underestimated Ms. Putnam.

She stroked the diamond-encrusted ring with the ruby-and-sapphire Patriots logo, and the engraved World Champions on the sides, so suggestively, he imagined that chalk-white finger with the spun-sugar-pink nails trailing up and down his dick.

And the damn thing rose at the X-rated daydream.

D scooted his chair farther beneath the table. He'd prefer to keep sexual harassment off the agenda this morning. Fortunately, the dining room was mostly empty right now, but in twenty minutes or less, the lunch crowd would start arriving. He cleared away the frog in his throat. Which felt suspiciously like regret.

"How does it feel?"

She fondled his ring and finger, and he'd never thought that a knuckle could be an erogenous zone, but her featherlight sensual caress was proving him wrong. He was getting harder.

"What?" he croaked.

"Having the tables turned."

D shifted in his chair, knowing he'd been given a serious reprieve. But her jab was another indication not to underestimate this woman.

He cleared his throat.

She pulled her hand away from his. "So, you want to start now?"

A particular shame cascaded through him. "I'm not crazy about interviews."

"I know." She nodded, her platinum hair brushing her cheekbones. "Why?"

A reason he'd never reveal.

D had a secret. One that if it got out could destroy everything he'd worked for—everything he'd built could disappear in an instant. And fantasizing about a reporter was as stupid as he wasn't. The way to avoid suspicion was to keep things light, keep the reporter off balance.

Jay had insisted that he needed to start giving interviews. He'd suggested Elise Putnam for several important reasons. She didn't have a lot of experience and she would likely go easy on him. And Jay got her this interview as a favor, so D was sure she wouldn't publish anything too damning. Not that D would ever let her get close enough to find out his secrets.

"I had a bad experience early on in my college days. Right pissed off my momma." While he had a reason for not wanting to let his secrets out, his mother's hatred of reporters made it easy for him to avoid them. She was not going to be happy with him, but this was definitely one of those "ask for forgiveness" situations.

She blinked. "You don't give interviews because it might upset your mother?"

Time to answer her question. D shrugged, his massive shoulders shifting beneath the custom suit. "I don't really understand why people need to talk to me. I'm just a guy who played football."

"If you hadn't been injured, you were destined to become one of the most accomplished wide receivers in the game. As it is, your stats for the years you did play are in the top ten for every year." That little frisson of awe in her voice tugged at him. She wasn't just reciting stats, her admiring words and tone made it clear she understood that his football accomplishments were impressive. Kind of a surprise. The Ice Queen didn't look like she would follow football, or any sport for that matter.

He puffed out his chest, proud of the fact that he'd made an impact during his short career, but still very aware that there were far bigger unsung heroes, and they should be getting the attention.

He shrugged again, his gaze shifting to the ornately carved mahogany wall that arced in a semicircle around an alcove. "It's just a game."

She cocked her head, and the tips of her hair brushed the upper swell of her covered breasts bringing attention to her femininity. Although he didn't think she did it to be provocative, he purposely kept his attention away from her luscious curves.

"You were groomed from an early age to be a football star."

Yeah, he had been. At the expense of other things. "I was lucky. I had coaches who believed in me and a mother willing to sacrifice everything for my career."

"Everyone knows your mother is important to you." There was soft vulnerability in her blue eyes, no longer ice, but warmed to the sweet, soothing color of the Adriatic Sea. For a second, he wanted to explore that hint of sadness and melancholy.

But he forced his attention back to the interview. His mother was important to him. Yeah. And he never, ever, ever wanted to disappoint her. "She is."

His momma he could talk about all day. "She worked two jobs and put aside her own wants and needs for years to make sure I had the tools to succeed."

"She sounds remarkable."

"Absolutely." D relaxed a little more as the pretty reporter lobbed softball questions about his mother.

Maybe this wouldn't be so bad. He'd work in some info about his new helmet venture and then meet with the event planner about his mother's surprise party.

Elise smiled at him, her eyes warm and her smile wide.

D analyzed that smile. Usually women fell into two categories. The women in one were nervous around him. Big. Black. Physically intimidating, because yeah, he kept in shape. He still did a demanding workout every day. Years of conditioning were hard to break. He was more than his appearance, and their fear of his size tended to piss him off, which just perpetuated that fear.

Or they wanted to have sex with him. Athlete. Famous. Ticked off boxes for a lot of women. He was a trophy fuck. Someone they could write about in their diary and slash a mark on their bedpost. And yeah, he might have reaped the benefits from that attitude when he was younger. But these days, he was ready for something *more*.

He wanted people…women, to see him as more than his celebrity or his size or his bank account. But he kept so many things private. He wasn't about to open up to a woman. And the type of woman he wanted wasn't likely to commit to a guy who kept secrets.

It was a conundrum.

But Elise Putnam intrigued him.

She didn't seem to be looking for a notch on her bedpost and she wasn't afraid of him. That combination didn't happen very often.

He signaled José and the waiter bustled over to their table quickly. D was feeling pretty good. He could do this.

D didn't open the menu. Didn't want to. "Give us the specials, please."

José rattled off the lunch specials. Then D ordered his usual. "Two grilled chicken breasts, house salad, oil and vinegar." He quirked his eyebrow and waited for Elise to order.

"Caesar salad with chicken and an ice tea." She handed her menu to José.

"Another drink, sir?"

"Why not."

D lifted his club soda and took a sip.

José gave a short bow, then left quickly.

She smiled again, and D began to wonder whether maybe there was a way to date her after this interview was over.

"You seem very attached to your mother." There was a wistful quality to her voice even though her face betrayed no emotion.

"She's my rock." He would do anything for his mother. Literally anything. She'd sacrificed so much to get him to where he was today.

"What did she think of you retiring early?"

"My mother supports me in everything." Which was why he'd never do anything to hurt her.

"That's so very…sweet." She smiled again, and a soft melancholy lit her eyes, making her seem more human, less frosty.

"That's me. Sweet."

She didn't take the conversational bait. In fact, she seemed a little choked up. That blank mask slid over her face again after a fraught moment.

"I'm assuming Jay explained why I was interested in doing an interview with you." He was really excited about this new helmet and the long-term possibilities for eliminating severe debilitating effects from concussions. "Too many players have career-ending and life-impacting results from concussion injuries. Not to mention that the sheer number of deceased players who test positive for CTE —chronic traumatic encephalopathy—in post-mortem autopsies is horrifying."

She jotted down some notes in her notebook and let D go on about the helmets.

When he wound down, she didn't start right in on the questions he wanted. "Tell me…how did you end up friends with Jay?"

He didn't need to ask her how she knew Jay. All the social register folks knew each other from their country clubs and their prep schools and strategic eugenic weddings where they only married each other and cemented hundreds of years of fortunes for the next generation.

He really wanted to emphasize his business. But he'd indulge this question. Charming her hadn't worked so he needed to be as affable as possible.

"A fluke."

She flipped through her notes. "Jay, Tracy Thayer, Diego Ramos, Peter Nguyen, Courtney Lee, and Duke Kalani. Are they all flukes?"

The BBC. He grinned. This he could answer easily. "Uh yeah. As a matter of fact, we all met at the same time." Total. Fluke. One that changed his life.

And this was perfect. He could talk about the BBC and then segue back into his helmets.

"We'd all been at a symposium and snuck out to a diner." Best decision of his life. He hadn't even wanted to attend but he'd promised his mother that he'd focus on his studies, so he'd reluctantly gone to the seminar.

"Playing hooky?"

"Yep. And it changed my life."

"Tell me," Elise said.

"It all started when I was a freshman at North Carolina."

Chapter Four

SPRING 2008, CAMBRIDGE, MASSACHUSETTS

D'ANDRE GLANCED AROUND GUILTILY.

It was pretty much impossible to be inconspicuous as a six-four Black kid while he snuck out of the Young Entrepreneur seminar, but he managed to slide out a side door as the speaker's attention was snagged by some girl in the front row who raised her hand every five minutes.

His head hurt.

Yeah, he'd promised his mother but even this dumb football jock knew that the guy at the podium was no longer on the cutting edge. He was taking about venture tactics that might have worked when D was in elementary school but the world moved at a crazy pace.

He nodded sharply to a Hispanic kid who sat on a bench outside the closely guarded lecture hall. Something about the guy struck D as dejected but you'd never know it from looking at him.

The kid stared at D's badge then sighed and stood.

A perfectly-groomed blond guy with shiny hair and the requisite country club attire of a navy blazer and tan khakis eased out a different side door. Huh, Richie Moneybags was cutting out too. He stopped when he saw D, then gave him a chin lift and a conspiratorial grin.

"I'm heading over to the diner across the street. Wanna come?" He was purposely slurring his words together, but even with the attempt to be ghetto, the prep school diction came through.

"Dude, that was lame." Some surfer guy sauntered up to them as the entire lecture hall came streaming out of auditorium for a scheduled potty break. He held out his fist and waited for a fist bump. "Duke."

D obliged. "D'Andre."

"You are a beast." Surfer Duke wore a suit and tie but his hair was silvery gold from salt water and he had mixed heritage olive skin with a killer tan.

"Jay." Preppy boy nodded at them both.

Jay's princess counterpart, the perfect preppy girl, bounced up to their little group. "Fabulous!" She clapped. "Let's go." She smiled at them all.

"This is Tracy," the prince said. They made a flawless couple like a prep school Ken and Barbie.

They all walked out together. D noted that the Hispanic kid trailed behind them.

When they entered the diner, a skinny little Asian kid sat at the largest table in the place, one of those with a booth and a weird circle banquette type thing and a chair on the end. His tag hung around his scrawny neck, and D had the random thought that he could crush the guy with one hand behind his back. But Tracy walked straight up to him and smiled. "Hi."

The kid blinked. "Uh, hi?"

"Can we sit with you? We're from the same seminar. We also decided we'd be better off trading ideas than sitting through more of that lecture."

"Sure?"

"Great!" She slid into the booth and basically herded him into the corner.

No way was D squeezing into that sitting area.

He grabbed the lone chair, turned it around and straddled it.

The Hispanic kid had followed, except now that he was closer D could see the guy was older than him and the golden kids.

"Peter Nguyen." The Asian kid chattered nervously, "I'm at Harvard. Graduated number one in my class but I'm already a junior because I took a billion AP classes." He paused, looked at everyone as if waiting for them to list their academic prowess. "Not really a billion, of course. I was attempting to be relevant. But clearly I've failed at social interaction."

And after that, everyone else said their names again with no mention of where they went to school or what their GPA was, thank fuck.

Preppy Ken said, "Jay Hollingsworth."

"The fourth," the bouncy girl added.

The Hispanic kid thrust out his hand. "Diego Ramos. School of life."

No apologies. D's impression improved.

"Why did you come here?" D wondered.

"Read about this seminar and wanted to see if I could get in." His posture was slightly defensive as if waiting for them to tell him to get lost.

Instead of being disgusted at his sheer balls, Hollingsworth the fourth's mouth spread into a wide, welcoming smile. "Nice. A rule breaker. Have a seat, Diego."

The chatty princess folded her hands in front of her and bounced on the seat. "Smart. You must be really motivated." She wasn't rude exactly but more like examining them all like bugs under a microscope as if they were some exotic unknown species that she wanted to study.

And maybe they were.

He'd bet that he, Nguyen, and Ramos were all foreign entities in her rarified world.

"Tracy Thayer." She gave a little wave.

"Thayer?" Nguyen asked. "As in— "

"Ugh, yes. That's my family."

Jay raised one eyebrow at Harvard boy.

"Understanding the political climate of my adoptive state is only smart."

He probably had plenty of time to study politics since he clearly didn't get out much.

"Let's focus on why we're here," Tracy said. "Entrepreneurs in training."

"I want to be a billionaire," Nguyen stated quickly. "But that seminar wasn't informative enough."

"Me too!" Tracy said.

"Money doesn't suck," Jay contributed.

Diego said, "I'm going to own my own business."

They all had large goals. No way was D going to admit that he was only here because of his mother. But as he looked around the table, he thought this band of misfits might be good friends to cultivate. And he was nothing if not friendly.

Before anyone could say anything, Nguyen blurted, "Hey, we're like the movie *The Breakfast Club*."

Five blank faces.

"The Jock, the Nerd, the Rebel," he slid a sideways look at Diego. So the Nerd paid attention. "The Free Spirit, and the Prince——" he stopped himself before he said Princess.

"Jesus, Nguyen. Do you ever get laid?" D snarked out. Peter Nguyen was the guy he couldn't stand. So crazy smart he looked down on everyone else.

He'd clearly hurt Peter's feelings. But shit.

Diego shot D a look. "Chicks dig smart guys. At least, according to my friends who are also crazy smart."

"*The Breakfast Club*…but the billionaire version," Nguyen said.

"We aren't billionaires," D was compelled to point out.

"Yet." Jay cocked his blond head and bared his white teeth in a cocky grin.

Of course, he was pretty much guaranteed to be a billionaire by the time he was thirty.

"Uh, the building we just bugged out of was named after your grandfather. Pretty sure you're a shoo-in." There went Nguyen, shooting his knowledge and showing off.

Jay flushed. "Family money doesn't mean it's going to come to me," he muttered.

Still, D couldn't even imagine that kind of money. He was seriously thinking about going into the draft in a few weeks. Then he'd be making more money than he'd ever dreamed of. He might not go in the first or second round, but it would still be insane amounts of cash. That's why his momma wanted him to come to this seminar. He wasn't about to be stupid with his money. But billionaire?

He'd just be happy to be able to support his momma so she could quit her jobs.

The surfer dude piped up. "Got to think big, man."

Yeah, but even D knew that what the seminar speakers

were talking about wasn't the future. So the Emerging Young Entrepreneur Seminar was a bust.

Even though Nguyen annoyed the shit out of him, D liked his optimism. Sitting in this greasy diner, he thought maybe he'd found his tribe. They all wanted similar things. Money, fame, acknowledgement. And he personally thrived on competition.

"Money isn't everything." Duke, the crunchy surfer dude, practically had *Berkeley pacifist student* tattooed on his forehead.

They all snorted.

Duke ducked his head. "Okay, yeah, it's important."

Diego pushed. "How about a wager, gentlemen…and lady?"

A feminine hand with black nail polish slapped on the Formica tabletop. "I'm in." The skinny girl from the back row with the multi-colored hair and multiple piercings tossed a smirk at Hollingsworth.

"You don't even know what it is," Jay argued.

"Doesn't matter." She shoved in next to Duke. "Name's Courtney. And this looks like the meeting to be at instead of the lame bull they're slinging back there." She jerked her head toward the building they'd left.

Jay tilted his chin in the air like a complete jerk. Weird since he'd been pretty mellow and open up until this point. "We didn't invite you."

"Oh, really. Who made you the head of this band of brothers?"

"And sister!" Tracy piped up, watching the back and forth avidly.

D tuned out Jay and Courtney as they bickered.

What could they wager?

"Guys, what's the wager?" Courtney kicked him under the table.

Diego said, "Okay, okay, first person to make their first million buys breakfast for everyone."

They looked around the table at each other, blinking, nodding.

"We need a name," Tracy bounced again, such perky, slightly annoying cheerfulness. "First rule of marketing is to create and stick to your brand."

"Billionaire Breakfast Club," Nguyen said stubbornly.

Billionaire. D had to admit, the idea was growing on him. He loved the sound of that. As he glanced around the table, the name was already sticking with everyone.

"All those in favor say, aye."

The chorus of Ayes was robust.

Everyone put their hand in the middle and bumped fists.

And the Billionaire Breakfast Club was formed.

❧

ELISE PROPPED her chin on her fist, enthralled by the change that took over D'Andre Smith when he talked about his friends. She envied his bond with those friends.

"Billionaire Breakfast Club, huh?"

He grinned. "It's good to have goals." Then he laughed, a deep belly mirth that spread out around him like happy dust.

While this was all interesting, that wasn't going to help her achieve syndication. This info wasn't enough as an angle for the article. She needed to dig deeper.

She'd gotten lost in his storytelling. He drew her in, and she wanted to join that camaraderie. The affection he had for his friends came through loud and clear.

"We still meet for breakfast once a quarter."

"I bet that would be an amazing fly-on-the-wall experience."

And with that he stiffened.

Shoot. For a few minutes she could tell he'd forgotten why they were having lunch—the more involved he'd gotten in the story, the more he relaxed he'd become—but her random comment had reminded him.

Elise shifted gears quickly, hoping the change in topic would loosen him up and garner more info. "How did it feel when you quit the game?"

"There's a point in everyone's career when hanging up cleats is inevitable. I had a good run and I'm happy with what I achieved."

And yes, she was pretty sure she'd seen that exact quote twenty times during her short bit of research. That answer was rehearsed and well-constructed. She was pretty sure it was also bull.

Hopefully later in the interview she could circle back around and ask him again in a different way. One that would achieve a more honest answer.

Chapter Five

THIS WASN'T SO BAD. ALTHOUGH FOR A FEW MINUTES HE'D
sort of forgotten why she was having lunch with him. She
was easy to talk to. D lamented again the fact that she was a
reporter.

Who knew that ice-cold blondes with a haughty streak
did it for him?

Elise Putnam asked a series of questions about what he'd
done right after retiring and he made sure to plug all his
contracted endorsements.

"Even retired, you rep quite a few commercial
products." There was a slight edge to her voice now.

"I only take contracts with companies and products I
believe in. But they're my bread and butter. Those
endorsements funded the seed money to start my sports
equipment business and my new venture. Not to mention
the exposure for charitable causes I support."

"Your philanthropy is legend. Most of your focus seems
to be on underserved kids."

It's what he wanted to be known for. "A lot of people

helped me along the way. I want to do the same for kids in similar situations."

Just one more plug and this lunch would be over.

"Let me tell you more about my company's new product. I'm particularly proud of the fact that we've developed a state-of-the-art helmet that's going to revolutionize diagnosis of concussion injuries and help with target treatment." The reason he'd agreed to this stupid interview in the first place.

"Just give me a press release I'm sure I can get the pertinent information from it." She dismissed his pitch with a wave of her perfectly French-manicured fingers.

"Our product will save lives and ensure that players have a good quality of life," he said through gritted teeth.

"Very admirable." She smiled, but something told him she was shifting gears, getting ready to jump him, verbally at least. She made a few more notes in her notebook. "Since I didn't have a lot of time to prepare before this interview, and so that I can get a full and informative profile for *Yankee Sports*, I have a list of other people I'd like to interview about you."

What?

She pulled out a list, added one more name, and then handed the paper to D. "I'm doing you the courtesy of asking first. It would be great if you'd allow access to the people on the list."

D sweated a little as she handed him the paper. Because he'd avoided interviews he wasn't sure about the protocol regarding her request.

"This is standard, I promise." She smiled at him, her gaze turning more quizzical as he didn't look at the paper.

"Why do you need to interview these people?"

"Typically a magazine profile relies on more than one

source for quotes and background information about the subject. I'm sure you've noticed when you've read articles about other people that the interviewer talks to more than just the focus of the article."

D's heart rate picked up. He hadn't necessarily thought this through. "But the whole reason for agreeing to this is to spotlight my new business."

"Which will be included. That's also why I added Jay and your agent to the list."

D looked at the paper in his hand, studied the list, probably longer than she expected. But one name jumped out at him. "You are under no circumstances allowed to talk to my mother," he bit out. "And I want my attorney to look at the list before I agree. Make sure that's on your tape. Not until my attorney looks at the list."

"Okay," she said slowly.

He tucked the list into his pocket. "I'll get back to you on the others."

D needed this interview over and done before she realized how uncomfortable he'd gotten in the last few minutes.

But before he could wrap things up, a raucous burst of laughter from the entrance to the restaurant blasted through his consciousness. Shit! He recognized that laugh.

D ducked down, the slatted wood partition kept him hidden right now but within a minute he was going to be busted.

"What's wrong?" Her perfect platinum brows arched down as she tilted her head quizzically.

Mary Smith hated reporters. Seriously hated them. "My mother," he whispered.

Elise lifted in her booth seat and craned her neck to look

over the partition. "Really?" Her smile illuminated their table.

Lordy, he needed her to not draw attention to them while he frantically searched for a reason to be here with her. "Don't look," he whispered.

She propped her arms on the table and hunched her shoulders so that she was below the partition. Her ice blue eyes danced with amusement, the cold demeanor wiped away by her smile. "Why are we hiding?"

"She hates reporters." Jesus, his momma would rip him a new one if she found out he was here with a reporter.

"You're seriously afraid of your mother?"

"Never piss off a Southern Black woman, she'll make you regret it." His heart pounded in his chest.

"What were you going to do when my article came out?"

"I had time to ease her into the idea of an interview." *Think, think.* "I've got it. Be my date."

She reared back. "Excuse me?"

But that was it. His mother knew all his top employees. His business was more like a family than a corporation.

He reached across the table and grabbed her hand. His forearm rested on her phone between them.

Her skin was impossibly soft. "Pretend to be my lunch date."

Her mouth opened. Closed. Opened again. "She won't believe it. You date gorgeous Black women, models."

True. And surprising that she knew that.

"God your skin is so soft." For a moment he got lost in the sensation of touching her.

She flushed, tensed her fingers, clearly ready to pull her hand from his.

"You're not kidding." In a heartbeat, she squinted her eyes, and her gaze turned calculating.

"Shit no, I'm not kidding."

"What do I get out of it?"

"The satisfaction of knowing D'Andre Smith owes you a favor," he hissed.

"Sorry, but I need more than that."

"Can we discuss after we deal with this?"

She smiled. "Sure, but you owe me."

His mother squealed. "Look who's here!" She grabbed his shoulders, but D kept his gaze square on Elise.

Please, he mouthed.

She blinked, dipped her chin.

D twisted around in his seat. In that moment, he realized he couldn't let go of Elise's hand. If he did, his mother would see her phone recording their conversation. Elise was trying to extricate her fingers from his grip, but he couldn't let her go.

"Hey, Momma. You didn't mention you were coming to Parker's."

She curled her arm around his shoulders and squeezed. "You either."

Love cascaded through him. He would do anything for his mother. "Ladies." He smiled at his mother's church posse standing in a semicircle behind her. There was a small hope that they would ignore the fact that he was with a woman. Very small.

"I raised you better than this, D'Andre Walter Smith. Introduce me to your…friend."

D still held Elise's left hand with his right. He couldn't afford to let her go. "Momma, this is my date, Elise Putnam. Elise, this is my mother."

Elise gracefully extended her fingers, putting her debutante training to good use. "It's a pleasure to meet you. I've heard so many lovely stories."

"Have you now?" Momma propped one hand with gold-tipped nails on her hip. Oh, he was going to get it from her. She shot him a censorious look that said they were going to "chat" later. "What you all doin' here?"

"Quick bite to eat," D said desperately. Sending a prayer to the God of Nosy Southern Baptist Mothers that Elise wouldn't blow it.

"She don't look like your regular dates." From anyone else that might be a criticism but coming from his momma it was actually positive. She'd been on him for a while to start getting serious. After years of caution about not getting a girl pregnant when he was young, she seemed to be on a mission for him to start dating regularly.

Elise's fingers tightened beneath his. "That's what I told him when he asked me out, but there's no accounting for the heart." She quirked her lips. Genius. She hadn't lied. She'd also acknowledged that she wasn't his usual type.

"I finally listened to my momma." D tried to butter up his mother. She eyed him suspiciously.

"Sure enough." Momma's lilting Southern accent softened the words to more of a *shore 'nuff*. "Nice to make your acquaintance."

"Enjoy your birthday lunch." D tried to verbally shoo his mother and friends along.

The bizarre tug-of-war between his right hand in Elise's and his left curled around his mother had him twisting awkwardly to hold on to both of them.

"You enjoy your—" Momma's narrowed gaze slipped to their joined hands "—lunch."

Momma and her friends strutted toward their table, which had a prime view of theirs. D finally let go of her hand, and shoved the recording phone toward her.

"Can you put that away?" D glanced at Elise's plate. She still had half her salad left.

She smirked. "Sure."

"Thanks for covering."

"No problem. But it's going to cost you."

"Fair warning. I'm a master negotiator. I have no misgivings about coming out on top."

Elise gave the side-eye toward his mother. She was right, she had all the damn power.

"Three more interview meetings."

Three more? "But—"

She wiggled her fingers at his momma.

"Okay, okay. But I get to pick the venues."

"How about we negotiate the first one now?" Elise took a dainty bite of salad. "I shadow you for a day at the office."

No way. "You shadow my morning routine before the office."

Of course the minx didn't outright agree. "What's your normal routine?"

"Morning workout."

Her gaze skimmed over his shoulders and down to his tapered waist. "What's tomorrow?"

"Weights." He answered without thinking, his brain stuck on the trajectory of her regard and wishing he was naked. *Bad idea, D.* He couldn't let her get the upper hand so he pressed, figuring she'd bail. "But you work out with me."

"You're on."

He'd been wrong.

He was a master negotiator. He had no misgivings about being able to come out the winner. Because that's what he did. He won.

Not this time.

Chapter Six

❧

Elise planned to avoid her father.

She had not gotten back to him on his approved husband list. She wasn't ashamed to admit she'd claimed a headache and informed the cook she was going to miss breakfast this morning. But as she left her room, she found a printout of the ten candidates her father approved of on the wood floor near the door to her bedroom suite. Someone, probably Franny, had slid the offensive list under her door. How humiliating that more people knew about his quest for grandchildren.

The list had read like a who's who of Boston's Social Register. She knew some of the men on the list. Nice guys, for the most part, but her mind kept going back to her lunch yesterday.

D'Andre Smith had a big personality to go along with his broad shoulders and exceptional accomplishments. The preppy white boys on her father's list couldn't compare.

She'd managed to score three more meetings with Smith so she could write a kick-ass profile on one of sport's most elusive figures. Rather than discuss the list with her father now, she snuck out the side door and headed to D'Andre Smith's residence.

Twenty minutes later, after clearing the lobby and taking the elevator to the top floor, she stood outside his door. An unexpected tingle spread through her while she waited for him to answer the bell.

She might have lost the initial battle with her father, but she'd scored against D. She snickered.

He'd gone into their negotiations overconfident.

Plus at the end of the day, he was the one with everything to lose. A fact she'd reminded him of multiple times until she'd gotten the better deal. Three more interviews.

He had tried to put her off by suggesting she attend his workout. She knew what he was thinking. She didn't necessarily look like an athlete. What he didn't think to ask was why she was a sports reporter.

She might be crazy, but after The List of Doom, as she had begun to think of it, it was more imperative than ever that she slam dunk this interview.

She tugged on the bottom of her spandex jacket and bounced on her toes, warming up her calves and hamstrings. They were going to be lifting weights, and she had dressed for maximum mobility.

She could admit, at least to herself, she wanted to show off a little. She'd been a collegiate athlete, competing in basketball and track. Their team trainer had given them a strict post-graduation conditioning program. Elise had kept up her lifting regimen while caring for her mother. Working out kept her from going insane with boredome and helped mitigate the depression that dogged her after her mother passed.

Between her workout and antidepressants, she'd

managed to stay on an even keel. It was probably time to give up the antidepressants but Elise couldn't quite cut that cord.

D'Andre yanked open the door, his phone between his shoulder and his ear as he finished a phone call. A key card in one hand and two bottles of water in the other, he hadn't looked at her yet.

"Give me one more second and I'll be ready to…" He jerked to a stop, mouth open. His broad shoulders filled up the utilitarian doorway to an exclusive condo right on the water downtown. She'd love to get a glimpse of where he spent his off time. But the heavy steel door swung shut, hitting him in the butt. He wore a red sleeveless muscle shirt and a pair of black spandex bike shorts.

"Ready to?"

He shook off his stupor, skimmed his intense gaze down her body, and then grinned. "Da-yum, you clean up good."

A pleased flush spread through her. Yeah, it was slightly inappropriate, definitely not scripted and clearly heartfelt since he spoke without thinking.

Then he blinked. "Uh, sorry. My bad. Didn't mean anything improper."

This wasn't a date. No matter what he'd told his mother. And yet, his unthinking comment gave her the feels. "I'll give you a pass this time. And for the record, workout gear isn't really cleaned up."

"Uh, yeah, but in that suit yesterday, your——" he made curves with his hands "——shape was hidden."

She didn't say a word. His more careful words weren't nearly as complimentary.

"I'll just shut up now." He double-checked that his door was locked. "So you're actually going to work out with me?"

"I thought we could do a little competition."

"What are we going to wager?"

"Whenever I win, I get to ask you a question and you have to answer."

"What do I get if I win?" The provocative banter hit her in the belly.

Whatever you want, the inappropriate thought popped into her head. *No Elise.*

She couldn't get involved with her interview subject. No, no, no.

But after yesterday's lunch she figured out what would make him agree. She cleared her throat. "Every time you win, I donate to the charity of your choice."

"Done." He rubbed his hands together and laughed evilly. "You ready to get your butt beat?"

"You're going down."

"Trash talk. I like it." He smiled at her, and she noticed for the first time that his smile was a little crooked, tilted up more on the left. His rich hickory eyes filled with appreciation and a deeper simmering lust.

They took the elevator down to the ground floor, where he unlocked a door marked private, and held the door open for her.

The gym was set up with two of everything, including a weight bench, squat rack, treadmills, ellipticals, bikes, and rowing machines. He plugged his phone into a jack over by a small fridge with a glass door, stocked with an electrolyte drink with his picture on the can. A deep dubstep beat reverberated through the room. Pretty fancy for a high-rise gym. The windows looked out on the Charles River but the coated glass made it impossible for anyone to see into the room.

"Wow, this is nice." The state-of-the-art room put her small home gym to shame.

"Thanks, designed it myself."

"Wait, this is just for you?"

"And my friends." He rubbed chalk on his large hands. Very large.

And her brain, which had clearly shorted out again, went to other things that might be large.

Elise snorted. Likely small. Although his shoulders and chest were wide, he wasn't bulky. But he was big enough that he'd probably taken steroids, which would have shrunk his balls to little tiny walnuts.

"You got something to say?"

"You ever take steroids?"

"What?!" He took a step back. "No. I don't—didn't—pollute my body with that shit."

"You're so big." And jeez, that sure came out breathless, sex kitten-like. And she was back at the beginning of the interview, when she'd first met him. Her breath caught in her throat.

His thighs were layered with muscle, his hips lean, but her eye was drawn by the bulge in his shorts. And oh dear God, under her gaze, the bulge was growing.

"What you ask that for?"

She jerked her attention away from his crotch, and flitted around the room, trying to come up with a way to save face. "For the article."

"Right." But she could tell he didn't believe her. "Quit stalling and show me what you got, white girl."

Elise picked up the chalk and rubbed the block over her fingers. "Three markers, bench, squat, and deadlift." She checked the weight on the bar. Way too much for her. But she could do close to her body weight. "Put one twenty-five on the bar."

"Uh, baby, that's a fuck ton of weight."

He'd done it again. He'd underestimated her. Elise couldn't help but be pleased. He wasn't going to know what hit him.

⁂

Shit. D didn't want her to get hurt.

"Spot please." She lay back on the bench and adjusted her ponytail. "I can handle it."

He'd like to give her something to handle.

But D kept that to himself and prepared to catch the bar if her arms buckled. He hovered over her, feeling a little silly.

"You sure? No interview is worth getting hurt over."

She rolled her eyes. "Just give me the weight."

And damn, even upside down she had a delicate ethereal beauty that pierced his heart. "Yes, ma'am."

In short order, she proceeded to do more reps of the weight than he'd expected. By the time she was done, her face was red, sweat sheened over her pale skin, and her eyes were a brilliant blue. She racked the bar and gave him a triumphant look. She still wasn't going to beat him but the fact that she could press that much was impressive.

He shook his head and dropped to the bench. "Where'd you learn to lift?"

Her form and her breathing exhales were textbook.

"I played basketball in college."

Hoops? He could see it. She was tall, close to six feet, maybe even a little over, and lean with sleekly defined muscles. D swallowed as his brain thought about how their bodies would lock together.

But he kept up the trash talk. "Basketball is for pussies."

"Seriously?" She hopped up from the bench and propped her fists on her hips.

"Sure, those skinny-ass guys can't hold a candle to the gridiron boys."

"You—" She punched his biceps then shook out her fist. "Ow."

"Told ya." He grinned. Too easy. He stepped back so he stood directly underneath a framed jersey.

She stalked over to Steph Curry's signed jersey, ran a finger along the wood frame. "You…you're teasing me?"

"Uh, yeah."

She stared in awe, not paying any attention to D. "You know Steph?"

For a chance for her to run her finger over his dick like she was caressing that frame, he'd set her up on a double date with him and Ayesha. "Met at a celebrity golf thing."

"Wow." She smiled. "Your turn, Hulk. Hurry up. I want to ask my first question."

The uptight woman who'd met him for lunch yesterday was gone. When she relaxed she was vibrant, energetic.

Which didn't matter because he couldn't afford to let her win any rounds.

"You know I can lift way more than one twenty-five." He added sixty extra pounds to each side and straddled the bench.

"Yes, that's why we're doing percentage of body weight as the measure."

His stomach dropped. The weight on his bar put him at ninety percent. He was pretty sure he would win.

Pretty sure.

D lay back and centered himself before gripping the bar.

Elise was positioned at his head. His brain went places it shouldn't and all the blood rushed to his dick.

"Can you spot the two forty-five?" he asked hoarsely.

"I got you."

D forced his brain to stop thinking about her and sex. He needed to win so he ignored her and stared at the acoustic ceiling tiles and focused on Jay-Z's beat. He did his set of reps with ease.

He racked the weight and sat up. Too quickly.

Shit. His head went dizzy and he dropped it between his knees.

Elise rushed around and bent over him. "You okay?"

Her perfume, just a hint of flowers, knocked into him. "Always feeling like I just took a monster hit when you're around," he muttered, embarrassed at his apparent weakness in front of this slip of a woman.

She huffed out a laugh. "Ha-ha."

"Pretty sure I won." He goaded her. He wouldn't have to answer a question. Unless…"How much do you weigh?"

"Never ask a lady how much she weighs."

He felt the flush start in his belly. His skin would hide his embarrassment, but yeah, he knew better. "Only way to figure out who won."

She groaned. Ha, she hadn't thought that through. "You're right."

"I got no problem telling you I weigh two seventy."

"Yeah but on men, more weight is a plus. Women get dinged if they're too hefty. With as many models as you date, I'd think you'd know that."

He shrugged. "I'm big. IDGAF what a woman weighs."

She sighed. "Well, in my world, it matters. Ladies do not discuss their weight or bodily functions in public."

"Okay, I don't even want to know why that's important."

She closed her eyes and did a quick calculation then blew out a huff of breath. "My bench was eighty-eight percent."

"My ninety beats your eighty-eight." He tipped up his head and did a little victory wiggle on the bench. "I win."

She was still hunched over him, and his movement brought their faces into intimate proximity. This close, the shards of silver in her eyes and the darker navy at the edge of her iris were clear. She froze, eyes wide, her breath coming in short little gasps.

D's heart thudded for an entirely different reason. His gaze dropped from her eyes to her sugar frosted lips, the cupid bow exceedingly sharp and shimmering with invitation. Her nostrils flared and she swiped her tongue over her lips. He'd never wanted to kiss someone so badly. To taste that cotton-candy perfection and suck her sweetness into his mouth, just inhale her feminine allure and dominate. Except somehow, she was the one dominating him.

"You slay me." He confessed.

Her exhale hit his lips. They held there on the precipice as if they both realized it was a bad idea, and still he didn't move.

Her eyelids drifted closed. But then she stiffened and that blank façade came over her face. He was beginning to hate that face. He had a feeling that was how she protected herself from the world. But she didn't need to be protected from him. He would never hurt her.

Before he could say so, she backed away from him and the odd moment was lost.

The trash talk continued as they competed in squat but D was careful to calculate the weight he needed to beat her again. So he was up two and they were about to start the third competition, deadlifts, when his cell rang. The small television screen on the wall lit up with his caller ID. "It's my assistant, which means I have to take this. He doesn't call me during workout time unless it's important."

"Of course." Elise wandered over to his signed Tom Brady jersey, and D answered his phone.

"Hey, Jamal."

"Sorry to bother you but the manufacturing plant wants some changes to the contract."

D got on the treadmill for his run. "Hit me. Give me original paragraph, then their strikethroughs. And I'll dictate my agreement or my changes."

Over the next thirty minutes, they went through the changes, most of them small, but one not so much.

"Strike out the added clause that they can move the facility out of the country if they're unable to find suitable factory conditions here. The helmets are to be made in the United States. Period. Preferably in an area that needs jobs."

"Understood."

"Okay, have the attorney look to make sure I didn't mess up the legalese and then shoot that back over to them this morning."

"Got it."

D ended the call and glanced down at the treadmill. He'd exceeded his usual miles by three while he'd been on the phone. He was also now behind schedule.

Elise had climbed on the rowing machine and was gliding through a decently intense workout.

Of course the interruption had seriously cut into their interview time. That was a bonus. "I'm sorry but I've got to get going."

D's phone rang again. His momma. He pressed a response button on his watch. He'd call her on the way in to work. But that made him remember that he'd promised Elise three meetings and he didn't renege on promises.

"No problem. Did you really just work on a contract over the phone?"

Her admiration was evident, which made D squirm. His stomach rolled, like the first time he'd been on Jay's boat, before he found his sea legs. "Uh, yeah."

"How?"

He tapped the side of his head. "Eidetic memory. I hear it, I remember it."

"That's amazing."

He thought about his life. His secrets. His shame. "It has its uses."

Chapter Seven

"Since you failed to rank your prospects, I took the liberty of arranging a date for you." Her father's shrill disdain cut through her.

"I've been busy." Avoiding her father, and weirdly mooning over D'Andre Smith. She'd had fun yesterday morning.

"Nevertheless, you're attending a function tonight as Alexander Weld's date. He will be here to pick you up at six. Please be ready."

She knew Alex. Sort of. They'd attended the same prep school. He was inoffensive and bland from what she remembered. But she had zero interest in marrying him.

"He's first on my list. Don't make a bad impression. The Weld fortune and his family's manufacturing facilities make him a logical first choice. His family would dovetail nicely with the Putnam brand."

As if she was a commodity to be promoted and sold. Her stomach churned but she kept her face placid, unemotional, calm. "I am not interested in getting married right now."

"That is not my concern." Her father folded his paper and straightened the cuffs on his shirt, dismissing her wishes without even a consideration for her feelings. "You need to get started on continuing the family name."

"Why now?" she burst out. Why was he all the sudden insistent that she become a brood mare?

He huffed out a sigh. "Your mother's death has made me face my own mortality."

Oh. At that her heart ached a little. Her father was the picture of health. As far as she knew he wasn't sick.

"And I want to have a hand in the grooming of the next generation." At this point he hadn't even looked up from his morning perusal of the news and the stock market. "Besides, I'd prefer that you were settled and taken care of before anything happens to me."

Sweet, sort of. Except he hadn't looked at her while making his explanation, and her father hadn't touched her with any affection since the day of her mother's funeral.

"I can take care of myself," she felt the need to assert even as she fumed.

"You run through your monthly allowance without a thought and have a job that wouldn't even support your shoe habit."

That's because the money was always *there*. But before she could defend her spending habits, he folded his readers, his brows arched down in a frown. "You aren't going out in *that*."

Her very short Nike running shorts and spandex halter top with the built-in shelf bra were perfect for running on a hot, humid summer day.

For the second morning in a row she was going to work out with D'Andre. Up until this moment, happy had been her primary emotion. And a keen sense of anticipation. She was looking forward to seeing him again.

They'd had fun yesterday. Even using percentage of body weight, she'd lost both rounds, bench and squat. But just barely. They hadn't had time for deadlifts. And since their workout had been interrupted by his phone call, he'd agreed to meet this morning as the second half of meeting number one. Today they were running, and she had plans to kick his butt.

But at her father's words, all that excitement and anticipation curdled.

Hurt, rage, impotence swirled in her gut but arguing wouldn't accomplish anything.

"I'm going running with D'Andre Smith. This is perfectly acceptable attire."

Her father's brows lifted. "You should just concentrate on getting ready for this evening and forget that ridiculous interview." He shook his head as if she were a stubborn child instead of a grown woman.

And thank you, Father, for once again managing to diminish me with as few words as possible.

Ten minutes later, D met her in front of her home. "Fancy house."

She slammed down the stairs. "Let's go."

"Hey, hey." He curled his fingers around her arm and she jerked to a stop. "What's wrong?"

"Nothing. Let's run." Rage churned in her gut. She needed to exorcise her feelings of impotence and focus on this interview. She couldn't afford to screw this up.

His palm was hot as he stroked her biceps. "I'm up two. Don't you want to know what you're going to donate?" His smile was infectious and for a moment she softened, but if she didn't move forward with this interview her life was going to be pregnancy and charity luncheons with a hundred of her fake friends.

She shrugged. "Sorry, terrible mood." It wasn't his fault her father was a dick.

"Tell me later?"

"Why do you care?" she burst out. "It's not like we're friends."

"Whoa." He lifted his palms in surrender. "Okay, okay. We'll run."

She scooped her fine hair into a ponytail.

"You want me to take a handicap?"

She shot him a dirty look. "You think I can't beat you?"

"'Course not." He stretched his quads one at a time. "Let's run."

"First one to the main thoroughfare wins." She tossed out. She knew she wouldn't beat him in a forty, she would bet his fast twitch muscles were still on point, but she hoped that his bulk would slow him down for a longer run. "Ready, Set, Go."

Ha. Elise took off. She was going to beat him and get a question answered.

Usually running soothed her. She would fall into her zone and the world would float away, her mind opening and her body taking flight. On a regular run day, she soared through the miles and her mind calmed.

But not this morning.

Right now she was all about proving herself. Proving that she could ask the tough questions and get them answered. So Elise pounded down the sidewalk, ignoring the old-money mansions and the neighbors walking their prissy dogs. Her feet thudded against the cement, her arms pumping back and forth, her heels kicking to her butt as she stretched herself past the point of comfortable. This was a death run, not fun, not a mere competition but one she had to win.

She considered herself a basketball player but the truth was she'd run on the track team too. Hoops was her first love, track was a way to stay in shape. Except she'd excelled at track.

No matter how hard she pushed, D'Andre's stride was longer and he stayed right with her, matching her leap for leap. She had to beat him. Had to.

"You realize I was a world-class wide receiver." His words were unhurried, easy, as if he wasn't working at all.

But Elise refused to even look at him. Her eye was on the finish line still half a block away. "Trash talk is not going to slow me down."

"I don't know, white gurl." He dropped back a little. "I might just let you win so I can watch your ass in those shorts. Day-um."

As his words registered, she stumbled, her brain tripping over his meaning. "What?" Without that hyper focus, Elise was falling. She was going to hit hard. "Crap."

"I got you." In a feat worthy of a world famous football player used to hitting the ground, D scooped her in his arms and rolled them onto the perfectly manicured lawn. They hit with a resounding thud, Elise on top, and they rolled until they were on their sides facing each other.

Her breath sawed in and out, her chest grabbing for air as she registered his arms cradling her tight.

"What did you do that for?"

"Only way to stop you from winning."

"You cheated!"

"I won. All's fair in love and war, baby." The husky endearment rolled off his tongue.

"So you admit I was going to win."

"I admit nothing." He laughed, his teeth white in his face, and that charming uneven smile melted her insides. "Besides, you got a sweet booty."

She was pretty sure no one had ever called her butt sweet, irrationally pleased with the compliment. She suddenly realized how close they were, their legs tangled together, his thigh between her legs, an unexpected intimacy in their position.

"We should get up," she said breathlessly as his cock prodded her softer belly.

"Gonna scandalize the neighborhood, lying on this lawn." He abruptly rolled so she was on top of him, and in a reverse push-up lifted her off his body and deposited her on the grass.

She sat on her butt, elbows on her knees and her swirling head between her legs. "Thanks for the save."

"Pleasure's all mine." He hopped to his feet, his muscular thighs flexing then bunching. He held out his hand to her.

Elise reached up and placed her hand in his. His warm fingers wrapped around hers as he pulled her to her feet.

"Who should I write the check to?" Defeat tugged at her. She was currently oh for three. And while she'd gotten to know D'Andre better, she still didn't have enough for a blockbuster story.

"I'm feeling generous. We'll call the run a draw."

"How big of you," she said drily.

"Right? I'm a regular philanthropist." He tipped his head back and laughed. His hair shook with his mirth. "So we got two hours tomorrow at the Boys & Girls Club."

"Hours? But…I'm going to donate money."

"Naw. We didn't settle on *what* you were going to donate. And I choose your time."

Elise opened her mouth. Blinked. Shut it. Because he'd definitely outmaneuvered her on this point.

Before she could draw enough air in to argue, Mrs. Kelly ambled past her. "Good morning, Miss Putnam."

Wonderful. This neighborhood fixture had been taking her morning constitutional every day since before Elise had been born. She was as old as dirt. Her baby blue Chanel coat and matching hat were a bizarre contrast to the very incongruous Nike walking shoes, her only concession to the uneven sidewalks and physical exertion.

"Good morning, Mrs. Kelly."

"I was sorry to hear about your mother."

A shock of pain pinged through Elise, her earlier lightness gone. "Thank you," she said quietly.

"She will be missed." Her soft tone disappeared, and she said briskly. "However, this does not excuse your behavior. People will talk if you keep rolling around on the lawn with a man."

Elise sighed, wanted to hang her head. Instead, she shifted her chin up and murmured, "Very true."

D tried to intervene. "I was just—"

"I know exactly what you were 'just,' Mr. Smith."

Wait, she knew D'Andre Smith?

Mrs. Kelly looked at D. Bit her lip. And still she didn't leave.

"Would you—" her eyelashes fluttered; was she… flirting? "—be so kind as to sign an autograph?" she pushed out in a rush.

"Of course, ma'am." He'd gentled his voice and somehow seemed far less intimating.

"Lovely."

Mrs. Kelly wanted an autograph? Elise's mouth dropped open.

The old lady eyed her. "Our family has had season tickets since the AFL merged with the NFL in 1970, miss."

Elise snapped her mouth shut.

"Have you got paper?" D pulled a sharpie out of a pocket in his tight shorts. If someone had asked Elise, she'd have denied there was anywhere he could have put it.

Mrs. Kelly carried a very small purse, but she managed to pull out a program with a Patriots logo on it.

D made a twirling motion with his finger, and Elise obliged by turning around so he could use her upper back as a writing surface.

"And who should I sign this to?"

Mrs. Kelly giggled. *Giggled!* "Eunice, please."

D hesitated. "Can you spell that for me? I don't want to get it wrong."

She spelled out her unusual name and D'Andre slowly wrote on the paper, the press of the sharpie deliberate against her back. Elise shivered.

"Thank you." Her smile was brilliant. "We've missed your leadership on the field. You were a great asset to the team." She nodded sharply. "But I'm pleased to see you aren't wasting your life now that you've retired. Your participation with various philanthropies is most impressive."

Elise wanted to laugh at the deer-in-the-headlights look on D's face. But she managed to hold it inside.

"Ah, thank you, ma'am."

She smiled serenely. "You two have a nice day now. And do try to refrain from shenanigans on the lawn in the future."

Elise and D silently brushed the blades of grass from

their clothes. Elise had her head down, watching the octogenarian until she turned the corner.

As soon as she was out of sight, D spoke. "Shee-it."

Elise put one hand over her mouth. She caught his eye. The twinkle was unexpected. And she burst out laughing. "Oh my God."

She laughed so hard her stomach hurt.

D grinned, his amusement completely taking over his face with his wide slightly crooked smile and his hickory brown eyes sparkling.

"That was…really nice of you."

D shrugged. "I'm well aware that fans are the reason I was able to rise out of my situation. Fans paid my salary and they buy the products I endorse. I'll always be grateful to anyone who's made my current life possible."

"You're a saint." The confession popped out without her thinking about it. But she had to admit that everything about him was positive.

"No. Just a man." His voice lowered, rumbled through her in a sensual rush. Her body reacted to the near caress of his voice over her nerve endings. Those inappropriate sexy thoughts were back.

And then he killed it. "What happened to your mother?"

"She died." Elise ducked her head to hide the rush of grief, and brushed the rest of the grass from her leggings. "Let's run back to the house."

"Hey." His barely there whisper stopped her more than the hand on her forearm. "I'm so sorry."

The lump in her throat made it difficult to speak. "Thanks."

The sudden onslaught of tears was unwelcome. Elise turned away and took to the sidewalk.

They ran in silence for a few minutes and she began to relax, her muscles loosening as they fell into an easy rhythm.

"What happened?"

"Cancer." She bit her lip. *Fuck Cancer.* Of course, a lady never used vulgar language.

"Fuck Cancer." He swatted at the air.

A burst of laughter bubbled up from her belly.

He glanced over at her, but he wasn't laughing. D reached out and grabbed her hand. He squeezed her fingers, and another swell of emotion rushed through her.

Her mother had been grace and dignity personified. The epitome of a classic beauty, she'd also been a force until she'd begun to wither away. And she'd surrounded Elise with love and acceptance. "I miss her."

"I imagine you do."

His relationship with his mother was enviable. And she knew he really understood her pain.

D dropped her hand as they rounded the corner and headed toward her father's house.

In that moment, D showed more compassion than her own father.

"Lightning round," Elise shot out so she didn't embarrass herself.

"What's that?"

"Quick either-or questions."

"You don't have a recorder."

"Trust me," she said, "I won't need one for this."

Her sense of victory was out of proportion for the small trust when he said, "Okay."

"Action adventure or romantic comedies?"

"This is some sort of trick, right? Action adventure. Ain't no self-respecting man saying anything else."

"Books or music?"

His gait hitched for a second, then he responded easily, "Music. R & B and rap are my favorites."

"Jay-Z or Beyonce?"

"Toss-up. Queen Bey, she's got it goin' on." He grinned. "I'm getting the hang of this."

"Fall or spring?"

"Football season, of course."

Chapter Eight

D SHRUGGED INTO THE JACKET OF HIS CUSTOM-MADE
tuxedo and tugged on the cuffs.

The silk draped over his shoulders and hugged his torso
like a lover.

Bad analogy. Because immediately his brain went to
Elise Putnam. He could not afford to think of her that way.
She wasn't a date, she was a reporter, which put her firmly
in the off-limits category.

His mind should be on tonight's high dollar
fundraiser, but instead he couldn't forget Elise Putnam's
sad eyes.

Her mother was dead.

He couldn't let her melancholy get to him. She was still
the enemy, or at least someone he couldn't afford to get
involved with. Even if she did intrigue him.

Forty minutes later, D stood among the crème of Boston
society, beer in his hand, trying hard to at least pretend to be
engaged in the conversation between two major donors.
They had donated significant funds to his burgeoning
foundation program to raise money for baseline IMPACT

tests in poorer areas and supply his concussion helmets to underserved communities.

His marketing and events coordinator had a bigger fundraiser open to the public set for later in the year but tonight's fundraising cocktail party was small. An intimate event where he could properly thank everyone involved for their help in getting this venture off the ground.

The two men waxed poetic over his prime football days, lamenting the fact that he'd hung up his cleats. Forget that if he'd kept playing he'd be putting his health and his brain in jeopardy. Now he was off the entertainment table.

D smiled tightly and wished he were somewhere else.

But donors were donors.

"Thank you very much for your contribution to the Impact'D foundation." He gripped the elder man's thin, soft hand in his and squeezed gently.

Beside him Stacey, his date and one of the hottest R & B singers on the charts right now, gave him a strained smile. They'd met last week after her performance at a benefit to raise money for music education in the schools. Introduced by mutual friends, she'd been somewhat aggressive in pursuing him, so he'd invited her to this event. On paper, they were a good fit.

Dressed in a shimmering column of bronze, her breasts were nearly spilling from her deeply cut V-neck with the spaghetti straps. She was gorgeous, accomplished, and he'd been moderately interested but their conversation had been...tepid, at best.

Most of the men here were drooling over her voluptuous figure so prominently on display. But D couldn't seem to work up more than a cursory appreciation for her very "in your face" attire and her smoking hot body.

Not to mention she seemed to have little sense of humor,

and as her gaze skated around the private event room at the Boston Harbor Hotel, he got the sense that she was as unenthused as he was.

Their mutual acquaintance sidled up to them. "Can I steal your date away?"

D smiled, trying not to let his relief show. Thankfully when he'd invited Stacey he suggested she bring her friend since he would have to work the room. "Of course. I need to mingle and make sure I touch base with all the donors."

As Stacey and her friend turned to go, a sleek dress of cream lace and a waterfall of platinum hair drew his eye. The neckline demure, almost chaste, Elise Putnam was the picture of understated elegance and an old-world femininity. There was nothing flamboyant or attention-grabbing about her, and yet he couldn't seem to tear his gaze away. She should have blended into the background but instead radiated a calm, serene poise.

He'd bet his size 2XL jersey that most people only saw an ice princess but there was a fire beneath her classic demeanor that burned bright, if only for him.

Her date, a typical frat bro who lived off his daddy's money, had a grip on her elbow. D's gaze narrowed because his hold didn't seem courteous but more proprietary.

The sudden surge of jealousy took him by surprise.

Before he could even think about what he was doing, D made a beeline for Elise and her date.

"D'Andre Smith, thank you for your donation." He thrust out his hand.

"Alex Weld, III." The guy eagerly shook his hand, angling his body so that he blocked Elise from D's view. D wanted to physically pick the guy up and move him. Probably not a good impulse.

"Elise. Nice to see you."

"Hi, D." Her tight smile loosened, evened out. A sparkle lit her ice-blue eyes. "Good crowd."

"Wait. You know each other?"

"I'm interviewing D'Andre for an article," Elise said smoothly.

"Ha. What'd you have to do for that interview?" The stupid guy realized his blunder as soon as it came out of his mouth. He cleared his throat. "Sorry, D."

The familiar "D" set his teeth on edge. "I believe you meant to apologize to Elise." D had made his silhouette bigger.

"Uh, yeah, my mistake."

Douchebags like this guy annoyed the shit out of him. But at the same time, he was here, which meant he'd ponied up fifty grand a person. And suddenly his last name registered. Weld. "Weld Manufacturing?"

"Yep." Alex Weld smiled. They were about to be in business together. Unless Weld Manufacturing tried to renege on the contract provisions specified.

But D would bet the diamonds in his super bowl ring this kid had no clue what was happening between their companies.

"You didn't mention you'd be coming tonight," D said to Elise.

Elise flushed, so slightly that if he hadn't been watching closely he wouldn't have noticed her discomfort. "It was… last minute."

"Well, thank you for supporting a great cause."

"Looks like the event is going well." Elise looked around the crowded banquet room.

Before D could answer, her date interrupted, "Another boring pointless fundraiser. You people are always looking for a handout."

Weld dismissed D'Andre's passion with a flick of his wrist.

You people? D's ire rose. *Don't piss off the donors, don't piss off the donors.*

Alex Weld took a hefty gulp of top-shelf scotch. "So, can you hook me up with an autograph from Tom?"

"He couldn't make it tonight." Most of his former teammates were at training camp besides which they supported his cause in other ways.

"Money is no object." He leaned in toward D as if they were friends. Not likely. The waft of alcohol coming off him could make D drunk. "I can pay for it."

There was something in his voice that put D on high alert. D's smile was tight. "This isn't the kind of night where things are auctioned for sale to the highest bidder."

The guy shot Elise a disdainful smirk. "Everything is for sale."

She flushed.

"I'm headed to the bar, you want anything?" Her date was apparently bored with the conversation now that he couldn't get what he wanted.

Her easy smile disappeared. "No, thank you."

He shot toward the bar like his Armani tux was on fire.

"Charming guy."

Her back stiffened and her chin lifted. "Are you pleased with the turnout tonight?"

"That sounds suspiciously like an interview question."

"If the request for a sound bite fits."

He couldn't forget that her main objective was a story. If he could control the message, then he'd be happy.

He grinned. "Yeah. This fundraiser is also a soft launch for the helmets we're going to be manufacturing." He clasped her elbow and she shivered as he led her to the table displaying prototypes of his helmet and literature for the company. "I'm hoping you'll pimp the company and the foundation in your article."

She relaxed in his hold. "Happy to."

"The ultimate goal of the company is to support the fundraising arm to get IMPACT testing and concussion detection into sports programs in underserved areas."

"That's a wonderful goal."

"What's with dickhead?"

She snorted, then covered her mouth. "You can't call him that," she whispered.

"I can do whatever I want." This was why he hated interviews and reporters. "Careful, or I'll think you share his views."

"As a former athlete, I think the helmets are a great idea. But you can't afford to outright disrespect people who have the wherewithal to fund your dream."

"Just because he has a shit ton of money doesn't mean I have to be nice." However D resented the fact that she wasn't completely wrong. "I refuse to compromise my principles for money."

"You're an incredibly lucky guy then."

Now it was his turn to snort. "Like you need to worry about money."

She blinked. That mask, one he now recognized and was coming to hate, dropped over her face. "You're right, of course. If you'll excuse me."

And she ghosted away, while he was still wondering what exactly he said wrong.

ELISE HEADED toward the women's restroom, needing a moment. Her date was turning out to be pretty much of an asshole. She didn't remember Alex being so insensitive when they were younger, but he definitely was now.

She slipped into the sleekly designed bathroom and then into an empty stall, lost in her own thoughts. Turmoil. Dread. Fear.

Because D was wrong.

She had no money. She'd been living with her parents, taking care of her mother and not working for the past few years. Her job with *Yankee Sports* paid minimum wage, which was fine while being supported by her father and a small trust fund allowance. No, she hadn't watched her pennies, because she'd never needed to before.

But now that her father wanted her to get married and start producing babies, she needed to pay attention to her finances so she could afford to move out of that oppressive house.

And D was right. She wouldn't need to worry about money…in three years. But until that time, she was dependent on her father for shelter, food, and any other basics. She didn't have a car. Her breath got a little short, lungs tight, when she contemplated how screwed she was.

She needed to prove herself with this interview. She needed to put aside her typical reluctance to the more invasive aspects of journalism and really dig into his life. So what if her stomach was a ball of stress? This event was the perfect venue to gather more information on D and she need to get to it.

Panicking in the ladies' room isn't helping.

Someone shoved open the main door to the bathroom.

"Girl, that brother is hot."

"I certainly wouldn't throw him out of bed for eating

crackers," a throaty voice murmured. Then she snorted. "If I could get him into bed."

And that was it. She didn't really want to listen to someone else's sexual woes.

Elise took a deep breath and headed toward the sink.

But as she turned on the tap, she realized the speaker was D'Andre's date, Stacey Jackson. She was stunning as she dabbed a rich gloss over her lips. Her bronzed skin shimmered and her dress was a miracle of construction, nearly hanging on her breasts.

If this woman couldn't get him into bed, Elise would never have a chance. And what was she thinking? She didn't want to have a chance with him.

"Maybe he's gay," Elise blurted out.

"Bitch, he *isn't* gay." Jackson laughed huskily.

Elise jerked back. "Sorry, I couldn't help but overhear."

"Private conversation," her friend said. The mood in the room had turned frosty.

"My apologies." Of course he wasn't gay. When she'd been on top of him this morning, there'd been a moment where an intense arousal simmered in the air around them.

Stacey Jackson raked her gaze up and down Elise's pale form, then turned away.

Elise headed out to find more donors to pump for information about D'Andre. He'd judged her. But she needed to put aside her natural compassion for his privacy and find out what his secret was.

So far, he was kind to old ladies, concerned about the fate of youth athletes and professional ones, thankful for his rabid fans, and competitive. And apparently, he hadn't had sex with his gorgeous date.

Nothing that would make a shocking exposé. But there had to be something.

Chapter Nine

D had mingled with everyone at the fundraiser.

The DJ was spinning a variety of socially appropriate tunes. He rolled his eyes, wishing for some head-banging dubstep beats to pound out the low level of discontent simmering in his chest.

Stacey was pressed up against him, her body moving sinuously against his. If she wasn't careful, those tits were going to slide right out of the silky column. She was sex personified, but damn if his gaze didn't keep searching out a very sleek body clad in modest lace.

"You up for some company later?" Stacey purred in his ear. "Hmm?"

Shit. His mother had just found Elise. They hadn't really discussed Elise continuing to mislead his momma. He still hadn't fessed up to her.

He wanted to wait until after her big birthday bash. Two more weeks and then he'd tell her all about the interview. She knew how important this helmet venture was to him.

Uh-oh. Mary Smith had a hand on her hip.

Not a good sign.

Stacey licked his earlobe.

He fought the urge to jerk away. "This is a business function. I'd appreciate it if you don't do that."

"Never thought you'd be such a fuddy-duddy."

"This is venture is very important to me, and it's important that I conduct myself with a certain propriety in front of my donors." He kept his gaze on his mother and his…reporter, watching the body language.

"Maybe she was right and you're gay."

Finally, her words penetrated.

"Da fuck?" He glowered. "Someone said I was gay?"

"There is nothing wrong with being gay."

"Of course there isn't," he shot back. "But I'm not. Who said I was?"

"Some white girl in the bathroom." She shrugged negligently, her spaghetti strap falling off one shoulder, the glittery dress hanging on an erect nipple.

He should be popping a huge boner. Instead….

Nothing.

They swung around on the dance floor and he gritted out through clenched teeth, "Is she still here?"

As if she finally got that D was pissed, she nodded mutely. "She's talking to your mother." She sniffed.

His mother had been less than impressed by his date. Apparently that feeling was mutual.

D danced Stacey to the edge of the floor and bowed. "Thanks for the dance."

"But that's all I'm getting tonight?"

D hesitated. He really had no interested in the shit hot woman in front of him. None. "Yes." He fought the urge to apologize.

"Well, thanks for the honesty, I guess." She gave him a cocky look.

"Thank you for attending with me."

"You're missing out. You could have had this." She ran a sharp tipped fingernail along the curve of her body. "Your loss, Smith."

He bowed out graciously. "I'm sure it is." But he didn't care.

D'Andre headed for the woman causing him no end of trouble. He got waylaid a few times by well-meaning investors, but he kept the two women in his peripheral vision. Elise and his mother seemed to be having a rather spirited discussion, and the thoughts of what they could be talking about caused acid to swirl in his gut.

By the time he got to the opposite side of the dance floor, Elise and his mother were laughing like old friends.

"There's my boy," his momma said with a wide smile. "I like this girl."

Elise flushed. Her mouth snapped shut.

D was a little surprised. But no matter how much he and his mother liked her, Elise was off-limits for multiple reasons. But his mother didn't know that.

"She's got substance."

"That's very kind of you, Mary."

D agreed. His mother was usually a little critical of his dates.

His mother had forgone her typical bright colors and wore a white sheath dress with a high neckline. Together they were polar opposites. The deep brown of his mother's skin contrasted with Elise's almost ethereally pale skin.

"Can I get a photo?" A young kid with a camera and giant lens, almost as wide he was, indicated they squeeze in.

"I'll get out of the way," Elise began.

But his momma pulled Elise between them and she had no choice but to smile.

"Put your arm around the girl, D," Momma ordered.

D curled his arm around Elise's back, curving his palm into the dip in her waist. She was covered from her collarbones to her calves, the dress sexy in a very understated way. The lace clung to her breasts and hips and thighs before swirling around her ankles. Unlike with Stacey, whose charms were blatantly displayed, D would have to work for Elise's secrets. And shit did he want to work for them. His attention was drawn to the heated shadow between her breasts, not large but they would fit in his hands perfectly.

She was solid, tall, with hips wide enough to handle him.

He could picture their hands twined into one, light to dark, yin to yang as they blended together in a haze of lust.

A delicate scent rose from her heated skin, and her pulse fluttered in the hollow of her throat. He wanted to think she was as affected by his proximity as he was by hers.

Her fist clutched the back of his tux.

The flash blinded him.

"Thanks everyone." The photographer shuffled off to take more pictures.

D was reluctant to let go. But it was about to become awkward if he didn't. He finally took a step back.

"Damn reporters," his momma muttered. "Mother...truckers."

The smile on Elise's face froze.

D snorted. "Nice save."

His mother laughed, infectious and a tiny bit raucous, and the moment slid away. Thank Jesus.

"Well, I'm headin' out. These fancy parties with all the stuffed shirts aren't really my jam."

"I completely understand." But his heart swelled. His mother was still one hundred percent committed to his success, even when she would rather not show up. He grabbed her in a big bear hug. "Thanks, Momma."

"You know I'd do anything for you, sweet boy."

A trill of laughter exploded from Elise. "You must be the only one who could get away with calling this giant a sweet boy." She grinned.

"You got that right." Mary grabbed Elise's hands. "You need to come to my birthday bash."

D's heart about burst. *What?*

"I know I'm not supposed to know about it but come on. Your momma's got a nose for secrets."

Oh no, no, no, no. This was not good.

"Two weeks on Saturday, the Omni Ballroom. I will see you there." She hugged Elise.

And D might be a little crazy, but he thought that Elise held on for a protracted moment.

"Thank you for the invitation, Mary."

"It's a surprise," D finally sputtered.

"Not so much." Mary laughed. "Baby, you should know you can't keep secrets from your momma."

Shit, when she found out Elise was a reporter, she was going to be pissed. D started to sweat just thinking about it. Quick, he deflected. "So what were you two talking about?"

"She was asking about what you were like as a little boy."

She'd been pumping his mother for information? Really?

D saw red. But if he gave in to that anger right now, his mother would want to know why and then he'd have to reveal that Elise was a reporter.

"Can I have this dance?" D held out his hand.

"Oh, I'm not much of a dancer," Elise demurred. "Especially not like your date."

Oh yeah, his date. He'd been so surprised that his mother was having a good time—she tolerated these functions for his benefit—that he'd momentarily forgotten that Elise had apparently suggested he was gay. Was she trying to invent a story for fuck's sake?

His mother came to his aid, nudging Elise toward him. "I'm sure you'll do fine. Go dance with my boy."

Elise gave in graciously and D tugged her onto the dance floor.

The DJ switched to a slow song, "All of You" by John Legend. He loved this song. Hopefully the next few minutes wouldn't ruin it for him. D yanked her body to his, the simmer of anger was a rolling boil now.

He had several things to discuss with her.

"You were interviewing my momma without her consent," he grit out.

"No! I would never do that." She stiffened in his arms. "We were just having a nice chat."

"What did she say?"

"That you were driven, intense."

Yeah, he had been.

"She said you knew from an early age that football was your way out of the financial position you grew up in. And that you were determined to give her a better, easier life."

The admiration in her voice soothed his ire.

"I was."

"That's an admirable thing. So why are you so upset that she told me?"

"My momma's life was hard. I don't need you bringing up my childhood and bringing it all back. She's got a good life now and that's all that matters."

"It's a huge part of your appeal to your fans." Her gaze sharpened. No way was he going there.

She was not going to dig up any dirt on him.

"Speaking of which, you told my date I was gay?"

She jerked, then blushed a fiery red. "Not exactly."

"What exactly?" he asked silkily.

He didn't necessarily give a shit if someone thought he was gay. On the other hand, he cared if she did.

"She was talking about you with her friend."

Huh, D had made a mistake there. One of the reasons he dated women celebrities was they were used to protecting their own private lives, which meant they protected his as well. Not that he let them get too close.

"She may have mentioned that you hadn't tried to get her into bed."

"I don't have sex with every woman I date," D bit out. "I like to know their brains before I explore their body."

"Oh," Her voice was breathy, and her pupils expanded. With that one little exclamation, he took note of other details. She swayed slowly, her body brushing his lightly, her breasts mere inches away from his chest. That delicate scent, some flower, rose from her flushed skin.

What would she smell like aroused and panting for him?

He had an image of her naked and writhing, her skin gleaming with sweat, her expression open and erotic as she came.

Jesus. His cock swelled like he was a teenager getting close to his girl for the first time. And he pulled her tighter, so the rest of the room couldn't see that he had an erection.

"Oh," she gasped, more startled surprise than breathy arousal. Her gaze shot to his, and her lips parted on an inhale, their soft pink glossy with some concoction he'd like to see painted on his dick.

"Not gay."

Her eyelids fluttered down, hiding her expression.

"Definitely not." She settled against him as if they were made for each other. The valley between her hipbones cradled his cock. "So, what's that?"

"That?" He rubbed his jaw along the silk of her hair, then whispered in her ear. "Baby, if you don't know, then we've got some learning to do."

She tried to pull away but D held on tight, and finally her arms curled up around his neck. And they swayed together to the soulful song, the words striking a chord of discontent in him.

"What I meant is why me?"

She called to some hidden longing in his heart. But he wasn't about to say that to her. Most women were willing to use him for his fame, for his money, and even though she wanted the interview, he didn't get the sense that she would use him for anything else.

He didn't answer, couldn't answer without giving away his building fascination with her.

"Your date is sexy and gorgeous and glamorous. Pretty much everything I'm not."

The insecurity beneath her words surprised him.

He countered. "You're strong, sleek, and sensual. You're an athlete, you're refined." And she definitely wouldn't embarrass him by talking about their sex life, or lack of, in a public restroom.

"Thank you," she replied softly.

"And you make me hotter than a turf field in the summer."

With every explosive word out of his mouth, her body melted more against his.

Her breasts rubbed against his chest, the hard points of

her nipples telling him she was as turned on as he was. And the very tip of her ear was bright red.

And just so they were very clear: "You make me harder than a freaking goal post."

Every time he saw her, there was that moment of disorientation, where he had to remember who and where he was.

She laughed, pulling away just enough that he could see her ice-blue eyes sparkling with an intelligent mirth. "Football paraphernalia as metaphor for sex."

"Use what you know." He wanted to score a touchdown with her and since she exhibited that bizarre insecurity, he wanted her to know it. So D let all the things he wanted to do to her simmer in his gaze as he stared down into her eyes Her laughter faded as a sensual heat flared in her eyes. She wanted him too.

But she was off-limits.

A flash blinded him, breaking their connection.

Elise ducked her head, and once he was released from the tractor beam of their attraction, the rest of the room came back into focus.

The photographer had just snapped a picture of them lost in each other.

As if she also realized the futility of wanting someone you couldn't have, they stepped back from each other.

"Thank you for the dance," she said far too formally.

"My pleasure." His voice deepened, roughened. Because that dance was as close as he was going to get to sex with Elise Putnam.

Off. Limits.

If only he could convince his dick.

ELISE'S NIGHT just got worse and worse.

Her father's choice of potential future husband—God, she wanted to puke—was drunk. Not falling-down drunk, because that would be in poor taste, but drunk enough that he swayed like a mini leaning tower of Pisa.

They waited for Alex's Porsche by the valet outside. Pretty fairy lights twinkled in the trees along the boulevard. They were tucked in the dark while they waited, and his hands roamed her body, skimming over her ass, his actions concealed by the dim lighting.

"Can't wait to get you back to my apartment and take you for a test run," he said in her ear.

"I beg your pardon." Elise swatted at his hands, trying to move away from him, but he had a tight grip on her forearm.

"Lady in the streets, freak in the sheets." His other hand squeezed her ass. "At least that's what I'm hoping. All that butch basketball paid off—your ass is firm as fuck."

She continued to try to extricate her arm from his hold without making a scene. "You really think I'm going to have sex with you tonight?" she hissed.

"I'd like a little somethin' somethin' for my time."

For his time? He'd spent most of the night at the bar or ignoring her. "Why'd you even go out with me?"

"You aren't the only one whose daddy controls the money." He snarled, "I'm as trapped as you are."

For a moment, she felt a tug of sympathy for Alex Weld. They were both in an unstable situation. But then he started talking again.

"If I'm going to have to have children with a woman my parents pick out for me, I'm damned sure going for someone who fucks well." He raked his gaze up and down her body.

Elise needed a shower at the pure greed in his perusal.

"You clean up nice. And all that Putnam cash works for me."

His car had arrived. Alex jerked her arm, tugging her toward the waiting sports car.

She was…speechless. "You're hurting me." She didn't want to make a scene; the truth was she could break his hold and incapacitate him with one slick twist of her wrist. But Putnams did *not* misbehave in public. While no one else was out here, she couldn't be sure that someone wasn't watching from the second-floor windows.

No way in hell was she getting in that car with him.

He shouldn't be driving.

She was still trying to discreetly take care of the problem when the air behind her shifted.

"Lady said no." D's deep voice rumbled.

Fabulous, and now her humiliation was complete.

"They all do, at first." Those chilling words stopped her cold.

D said silkily, "Not if you're doing it right."

Alex was too drunk to hear the edge in D's voice, but Elise heard it loud and clear.

He lifted a lazy hand and signaled to the valet. "Get the man a cab and park his car again."

"Yes, sir." The kid nodded eagerly.

"Thanks, my man."

"My pleasure, Mr. Smith."

"I'm not taking a cab," Alex said belligerently.

D bent down to Alex's ear and whispered something to him as the cab pulled up. The valet opened the door and poured the drunk asshole inside.

D gave her a choice. "You want to go with him?"

Elise stood there frozen. Hell, no. But she realized she didn't have any money or a credit card for a cab, and her procrastination about putting the Uber app on her phone was a seriously bad oversight right now. "No," she whispered, thinking frantically.

He slammed the cab door shut, and the yellow taxi pulled away from the curb.

Elise watched in a detached haze as her means of getting the four miles from downtown out to Brookline disappeared into a sea of taillights.

"What's wrong?"

A kind of weird shame enveloped her. Reaction from the multitude of things that D'Andre Smith had inadvertently saved her from sweeping through her in a burst of adrenaline. "I—I—" Her teeth began to clack against each other, the clatter loud in the silent night and a subtle shake started in her bones and radiated outward. Cold. She was so cold.

So…alone.

And then D wrapped his arms around her.

A sudden and unexpected peace flowed through her. Just for a second, Elise rested her head on his chest, the comforting boom of his heart beneath her cheek. She tucked her head against his neck. Just a second, and then she'd figure everything out.

"Thank you."

He petted her for a few moments. Every soothing swipe down her back should have calmed her, instead the tension ratcheted into an unbearable tightness.

She…needed to go. Get the hell out of here.

The night had been a disaster. She hadn't gotten any dirt on D'Andre Smith. The man was a freaking saint. Her father's first choice—dear God, if Alex Weld was bad what would the others be like?—was scum.

Elise stepped out of his embrace and shoved out her

hand for him to shake. "Well, I'd better be going." She forced a tight smile to her face.

A Putnam never showed defeat.

D cocked his head, and his little twists waggled. "You gonna be okay?" He took her hand, his clasp easy, light and nonthreatening.

"Of course." Then she turned on her heel, oriented herself, and started walking.

Chapter Ten

D WATCHED THE GENTLE SWAY OF HER ASS FOR A FEW moments, marveling at the fact that her simple dress and tight body turned him on way more than the obvious charms of his date for the night.

Then it struck him. She didn't have a car. And the taxi stand was back here.

He loped up to her. "Where are you going?"

"Home," she replied softly but didn't turn to look at him, just kept putting one foot in front of the other.

"Elise, talk to me."

"I'll schedule the next interview session with you tomorrow when we can both check our calendars."

She continued to refuse to look at him.

He grabbed her forearm. And she winced. What the fuck?

"Stop, please. Talk to me."

Her back to him, he watched her stiffen before pivoting around. D lifted her arm to the dim street light. Fingertip-shaped bruises marred the perfection of her pale skin. "Did he do this?"

She flinched. Looked over his shoulder. "Probably."

"Jesus." He was still holding her arm, but gently. "Next question."

"Usually that's my bailiwick."

"No being cute." He inhaled and held it. Because he finally figured out that you had to ask the right question with her. "How are you getting home?"

Her lush mouth, lipstick worn off, the lips a shadow of their usual cotton-candy pink, tightened. "Walking."

That's what he was afraid of. He wanted to yell at her, but that was a bad idea. "I'll drive you."

"That's not necessary."

"My momma raised me to look after women. I'll take you home."

He signaled to the valet.

"Fine." She lifted her chin, clearly not about to show any weakness.

The valet roared up in D's tricked-out Cadillac Escalade. After signing an autograph for the kid, D pulled into traffic and headed for Brookline.

He was the charming one. The guy guaranteed to put a smile on your face because if he was charming the socks or panties off someone they wouldn't ask the hard questions. But he didn't have it in him to be charming right now.

There was a quiet desperation to her silence that ate away at his resolve to let her alone while he drove her home.

She was a strong woman. Why would she put up with that kind of treatment from a date? Why would she even go out with a guy like that?

"What gives with the douchebag?"

She grunted, a laugh maybe? But didn't answer.

And he didn't give up. "Why did you ever agree to a date with that guy?"

She tossed back, "We can't all date celebrities."

"We were talking about you," he said evenly.

"Your date was a bitch."

"She had attitude," he corrected.

"She was discussing the fact that you hadn't had sex with her in the bathroom, in public," Elise snipped. "Bitch."

"Fair enough." A slow boil simmered beneath the surface. He didn't like the fact that his date had been less than discreet, but the fact remained that Elise's date had hurt her.

He continued to push at her. Why? The Weld guy didn't make sense with what he knew of Elise. He couldn't reconcile the tough, assertive woman who was interviewing him with the meek, almost subservient woman who'd let that prick treat her like shit.

What was she hiding? And why the hell did he care so much?

He glanced over at her, the overlarge black leather seat seeming to swallow her up until she looked almost fragile. He softened his voice, "Why?"

"I didn't have a choice."

"What do you mean?"

"I'm being auctioned off to the highest bidder," she said bitterly. "I'd think you'd have a fairly good grasp of what that means."

He couldn't wrap his brain around what she was saying. "But…thought you rich folk all had trusts and shit."

She flushed. "I'll be able to access my trust when I'm twenty-seven. Until then I'm dependent on my father unless I can make enough money to support myself."

"How long until then?"

"Three years."

Jay-sus she was young. And yet the look in her eyes was ancient.

He didn't have the patience to find a delicate way to ask so he went for it. "Why don't you have a career already?"

"I've been caring for my mother for the last two and a half years."

He wanted to touch her, place his palm over her clenched fists and give her comfort. But he was aware that she seemed poised on a knife edge, holding it together. One wrong move and she would shatter. He didn't want to be the one to push her over that edge.

"I'm sorry about your mother."

She sighed. "She was really sick at the end. She's at peace now."

"Doesn't make it any easier for the living."

She smoothed her flat fingers over the lace of the dress, pressing out a small wrinkle over her thigh, then flattened her fingers until they were white with tension.

D made a snap decision. Instead of turning onto Storrow, he flipped his blinker and headed to his place. He'd soothe her until she was ready to deal with life.

"Can't you tell your dad it didn't go well? This isn't feudal England, after all." He knew a lot about expectations and not living up to them. "Your father has to care about what makes you happy."

She laughed cynically. "My happiness is not even in the equation."

D pulled into the garage without comment from Elise. Which showed how upset she was, she hadn't even noticed that he wasn't taking her home.

He slid into his parking space and turned off the engine. Without giving her time to protest, he got out and headed around the car. He opened her door and held out hand out to help her from the car.

As if she finally realized that she wasn't at home, she paused, half in and half out of the high seat. "Where are we?"

"Brought you home, thought you could use a few minutes to recuperate."

"That's…really nice."

"We can hang out and when you're ready I'll drive you home." He grasped her arm to help her out and she winced. He'd forgotten about the bruises.

She stumbled against him as she slid to the ground. Her forehead brushed his chest and his arms went around her to stop her from barreling into him.

"I've got you." The whisper escaped before he could pull the comforting words back. She melted against his chest, and her breath soughed against his neck. His arms tightened around her, pulling her into the protective circle of his embrace. He wanted her.

But as the reality of where they were and who she was with hit her, she stiffened and pulled away. "You should take me home."

But all the conflict of the past hour caught up with her, and Elise began to shake.

"Let's get you settled."

"I'm f-fine." Mini tremors shimmied through her body and she shook against him.

"Come up and have a small drink. Tea, if you want."

She giggled and he liked that sound a hell of a lot more than the chattering teeth. "*You* drink tea?"

"Hell, no. I'd rather cut off my left nut than have a cup of tea."

"I pegged you as more of a he-man, put hair on your chest, coffee drinker. Grrr." She growled.

He smiled at her explanation because she was right. "My buddy Pete likes tea."

While he was distracting her, making her laugh, he led her into the elevator and they headed for the penthouse.

Finally she was steady on her own two feet, no need to hold her up anymore. Too bad he missed her weight and the trust that she put in him. Within minutes they were standing in his foyer.

Elise glanced around curiously.

And shit, he really hadn't completely thought this through. He let very few people into his private domain.

"So, this is the inner sanctum." Her smile revealed a curiosity but not an avaricious gleam or calculating glance as she prowled around his sparse living room.

He had a big sectional sofa that would seat his bulk comfortably. Two large armchairs flanked a small table with a light that cast an intimate glow throughout the room. An enormous flat screen dominated the wall across from the sofa, but D didn't actually watch much television. His stereo was kick ass because he listened to a lot of music.

The open-concept floor plan featured a large kitchen and eating area that flowed into the living area. Down a short hallway was the master bedroom and one guest bedroom. His condo had a very clean, very spare look.

He braced, waiting for her reaction.

Instead of asking why he didn't live in a mansion or have a giant condo, she headed straight for the wall of glass. "What a gorgeous view."

"Yeah," he agreed, but he was looking at her, framed by the city lights shimmering in the sky and reflecting off the surface of the river.

D followed her.

From her tiny purse, an old-fashioned telephone ring *brrring*-ed.

Elise jolted. She pulled out her phone and stared unblinking at the screen. But she didn't answer.

"Everything okay?" Something about her lack of reaction tipped him off.

"It's my father." She continued to stare at the phone.

"Elise, baby, talk to me."

She wrapped her arms around her middle, faced the cityscape, and hugged her waist tight.

D had seen her proud, defiant, laughing. The sweetness of her blush when Eunice Kelly caught them rolling around on the lawn, but he'd not seen her look this defeated. Even with the douchebag she'd been more pissed than downtrodden.

He wasn't known for sitting back and letting things happen. He was a doer. He had goals and he knocked them down. And right this second, his goal was Elise.

Her white-blond hair more brilliant than lights glimmering on the river, she drew him against his better judgement. His goal was simple. He wanted to make her feel better.

He wanted her.

He burned for her.

❧

TENSION IN THE ROOM THICKENED, turned syrupy. She was no longer thinking about her father. Instead, she was thinking about herself. About putting herself first. About grabbing what she wanted instead of being shoved in a direction she didn't want to go.

Unless she could find a way out, her life wasn't her own. She was beholden to her father, her family, constrained by his intentions. Her job wasn't going to be enough to get her out of her current situation.

Sleeping with your interview subject was frowned upon. It wasn't technically against the rules but ethically it was a bad idea even if her stupid boss had suggested it. But she was trapped in a situation that was only going to get worse. In this moment, she had the chance to take something for herself.

She wanted to explore this connection with D'Andre. To erase the sliminess Alex Weld's words had covered her in.

His reflection in the plate glass window, D hovered behind her. One could make the argument that he appeared menacing, but she had never felt more protected.. She held her breath, waiting for that first touch.

He stretched his fingers and reached out. But as if he'd changed his mind, he clenched his fist. She whirled around and pressed back against the window from her butt to her shoulders. "Don't."

"Don't what?" His deep voice rumbled thought her, setting off little detonations beneath the surface. "What do you want?"

"Don't pull away," she whispered. Then she deliberately placed her palm over the thud of his heart. His body emanated heat through his crisp white shirt. He was solid, real beneath her hand.

No hidden agendas, no treating Elise like an object strictly for his pleasure. He truly appreciated women. That was obvious every moment she spent in his company.

Now he was holding his breath. Her deep inhale brought their chests together, then apart. At the small brush of his heat against her breasts, her nipples hardened.

She hadn't had sex in…a very long time. And prior to that it hadn't been all that….noteworthy.

But she had a feeling with D those prior impressions would be shattered. He exuded an innate sensuality. He touched, he tasted, he moved, and all she could do was wonder if he approached sex with the same enthusiasm and curiosity that he tackled life.

She licked her lips, her gaze frozen on him as he leaned closer. His hand cupped her shoulder, and her sex wept for more. For him.

"You're killing me here, Elise." So close his breath puffed against her mouth, buzzing with a sexual anticipation.

He hovered over her as he searched her gaze, looking for what she didn't presume to know. Her eyelids fluttered shut at the intensity in his dark eyes. A deep well of sensuality churned beneath his low-key approach to life and his relaxed demeanor.

She should have known. He'd been a competitor for eight years in the NFL, and before that college and high school. Since he was in his teens, his goal was to win.

She wanted him to kiss her. To ravish her. To win *her*.

Instead of kissing her, he diverted at the last moment and skimmed his lips along her jaw. He pressed a long openmouthed kiss beneath her earlobe before nuzzling the shell and groaning. "You are driving me fucking insane."

His hands came up to clasp hers. He threaded their fingers together, and flattened the backs of her hands against the cool glass. Elise arched her neck, all but begging for a harder touch. She was trapped, her hands anchored by his. She bowed back, trying to find some other place to touch besides their hands and the light, oh so light, skim of his mouth on her jaw, behind her ear. His tongue came out to taste her skin. Sampling her as if she were his favorite treat.

"Damn, girl, you taste so good."

Right now she wasn't thinking about him as her interview subject, or searching for his secrets so that she could write a kick-ass profile. Because those things weren't important in this moment. Her only focus was D'Andre. She needed him. Needed what he could give her.

And he'd barely touched her.

Elise rubbed her breasts against the thick muscles of his pecs. He groaned and let go of her hands. She twined her arms around his shoulders and reveled in his hard to her soft.

With one large hand, he palmed her ass and pushed her into his erection.

His huge erection.

Her sex clenched, contracting at the thick bulge rubbing against the concave valley between her hipbones, and she moaned.

Elise's body was on fire.

He cupped his other hand around her breast and squeezed and shaped as if he were holding onto a football for touchdown. Every caress lifted her to new heights. But she needed…. "More."

D dragged his tongue down her neck, then traced the skin of her collarbones along the cream lace. That should not have been sexy but her body went up in flames. Finally, he pinched her nipple, and her sex flooded with arousal.

Elise tugged at the bottom of his shirt, pulling the tail from the confines of his pants. She needed to touch his smooth skin, force him to shiver like she shivered for him. She needed to feel the heat of him underneath her palms.

To surge against all that strength and let him conquer her body like he conquered the football field.

The slight scuff of his corkscrew twists was a sensual skim against the column of her neck. He glided his palm along the sensitive inside of her arm. His hands had calluses, no doubt the result of all that lifting he did to stay in shape.

She hooked her palm around his neck, pulling him toward her, needing him to kiss her more than she needed breath.

His other hand shaped her body, running over the arc of her waist and down her hips, until his fingertips breached the hem of her dress. He lightly dragged the tips up the back of her thigh, his touch electric as he activated zones she didn't even know were erogenous.

Elise explored the muscles of his back, his traps, his lats marveling at how cut he was even as she tried to direct him where she wanted him to go.

She pulled him close, because he allowed it.

His erection prodded her belly.

"You're so hard."

He chuckled against her ear as he traced the shell. "Baby, I'm just getting started." He scooped his other hand beneath her butt and lifted her.

She yelped.

"I'm too—" That finally got his mouth where she wanted it as he dove into a kiss.

Elise wrapped her legs around his surprisingly small waist and locked her ankles.

The move brought their groins together. Her panties were damp, the hem of her dress rucked up around her hips as he crowded her against the window. The cool glass at her back and his heat against her front created an incredible contrast.

Surprise, embarrassment, lust all competed for dominance.

Meanwhile his mouth devoured hers, their teeth clicking together. She angled her head to get closer, to taste him. He tasted like man and salt and maybe a hint of beer. Pure sex appeal. A slight floral scent mingled with vanilla overwhelmed her senses as he kissed the hell out of her. Her head filled with light enhanced by the feeling of weightlessness as he held her aloft.

D groaned into her mouth. "Jay-sus." He pushed his forehead onto the glass next to her.

"Why'd you stop?" Elise continued to kiss his jaw, his neck, nipping the hollow of his throat, any bare skin she could reach.

He panted. "Trying to slow down."

"No."

He still held her against the window, and she was not a small woman, his hands hot on her ass. He chuckled. "No problem asserting yourself now."

"Touch me," she begged.

She began to unbutton his shirt, desperate to be skin to skin.

With one fingertip, he stroked her through her soaked underwear. "Day-um," he breathed against her lips.

Her breath caught, her head swirled, dizzy with a truckload of lust.

Her fingers fumbled with the buttons, when he began to trace the edges of her panties, easing under the lace, his caress unbearably intimate, and he hadn't even really touched anything important.

Finally she had his shirt undone, and pushed it off his

shoulders. Elise kissed her way down the center of his chest, his skin supple and smooth beneath her tongue.

As she licked his nipple, his finger eased along her sex, and finally he touched her. He rubbed his finger through her curls, spreading her arousal. She bowed against his abs and the tip of his cock rubbed her through the barrier of his dress pants.

With a full-bodied groan that rumbled through him and into her, D let her slide down his body, until her pale ivory pumps touched the Brazilian wood.

Her dress was up around her waist and wisps of her hair distorted her vision. His chest gleamed a dark ebony framed by the crisp white tux shirt, the elastic band of his signature underwear peeking out of the top of his pants.

Hotter than the underwear ad he'd posed for—if the ad agency had taken his picture like this, they'd have sold double the product.

D's pecs bunched as he clenched his fists. Their chests heaved in unison as they stared at each other.

What next?

⬥

Fuuuccck.

He wanted her.

She leaned against his picture window, her hair mussed from his hands, her chest heaving, her jaw and neck pink from his beard, and her dress gathered around her waist, exposing her bare legs and elegant ivory lace panties.

D reached for the hem of her dress and began to tug it down. He couldn't take advantage of her when she'd been so upset.

Her fingers wrapped around his wrists, stopping him.

Their strength made him pause. He stared at her hands, so pale and delicate against his skin, the contrast between them never more apparent. And yet, he had a flash of images of those hands against his body, sending another rush of blood to his engorged cock.

He ached. His iron-hard erection pulsed against the restraint of his zipper, harder than he could ever remember it being.

"Trust me. I'm making a choice."

As if she'd read his mind. "You—" He cleared his throat. "You're sure?"

"I want this." She let go of his wrists and reached for the button on his waistband. She held his gaze as she opened his pants and pulled down the zipper. The conviction in her strained voice persuaded him. "I want *you*."

He still held the bottom of her dress.

Her chest lifted, and she held her breath. His gaze dropped from the intensity of hers and he took note of her body. Her nipples budded beneath the cream lace, and her cheeks flushed under the onslaught of sexual intensity. When he stared into her eyes again, bright desire blazed in her pale blue eyes—nothing cold or ice princess remained.

The silence in his apartment was absolute.

The only sound was their breathing and the thud of his heart.

He was a lot more discriminating than the press gave him credit for. Sure, he had gone through a period where he took advantage of all the free sex from football groupies and women who just wanted bragging rights for banging a football player.

But his mother had distilled in him a healthy respect for women. And for not getting a woman pregnant out of marriage. And…now was definitely not the time to be thinking about his mother.

Especially when Elise skimmed her strong fingers over the bulge of his erection then shoved his pants down to his thighs.

Her green light was never more apparent. And his momma didn't raise no dummy.

D curled his fingers around the hem of her stretchy lace dress and slowly raised the delicate material exposing the flat of her stomach. The higher the dress and his hands went, the more of her was revealed to him. Next came the ivory lace bra that matched the dress, barely there. The cups pushed together and lifted her breasts like an offering just for him.

She let go of his pants and raised her arms above her head.

He pulled her dress off and tossed it to the floor, realizing how exposed they were right now. He loved this view, and even though it was doubtful anyone had a telephoto lens aimed at his apartment, and the coated windows ensured voyeurs would only see silhouettes, he still wanted to protect her.

She stood there in a matching lace bra and panty set, with her pumps still on and a strand of pearls around her neck that probably cost as much as his Caddy.

Even as he was tossing her dress, she was following his pants down to the floor.

He toed out of his dress shoes, trying not to get off on her kneeling at his feet, her blond hair catching on his black boxer briefs and the fucking pipe of his erection.

The thought of watching her suck his cock sent another burst of lust straight to his dick.

But not this time.

Before she could make his vision come true, D tugged her to standing and lifted her into his arms and headed for his bedroom.

He shoved open the door with his shoulder, careful not to knock her against the frame. A single lamp on the nightstand cast the room mostly in shadows. D laid her down on the black comforter, the Egyptian cotton not nearly as soft as she was.

The skin above her bra shimmered, highlighting the plump mounds of her breasts, and a light floral scent rose from her heated flesh.

She lay on his midnight sheets like a sacrifice sent to the gods.

And that's what he felt like when he noted the blurry sensual look in her eyes. A god. And she was his tribute.

Chapter Eleven

ELISE MIGHT HAVE BEEN EMBARRASSED. SHE WAS SPLAYED
across his black comforter, exposed and open for him.
Normally she was a bit shy, but sheer appreciation shone in
his eyes as he took in her bared body.

He saw her the way she wanted to be.

Not Elise Putnam, the pauper heiress puppet, controlled
by her father.

Instead he saw the daughter who nursed her mother.
The athlete who was strong. The woman with fierce
determination and drive to stand on her own two feet. The
woman ready to move forward. To take what she wanted.

And right now, she wanted D'Andre Smith.

D ran his hands over her flesh with a bold assurance that
fired her mind as much as her body. Her experience was
admittedly limited. She hadn't had sex since college. Living
at home with a terminally ill mother tended to pretty much
inhibit intimate experiences of the sexual kind.

He bent his head and sucked her nipple into his mouth.
Right through the sheer ivory lace. The warm suction as he
tongued her created an answering tug low in her belly. Elise

ran her palms over his sleek, warm skin. The bunch of muscles at his shoulders and the bulge of his biceps emphasized how strong he was. He'd picked her up with little effort.

His black eyelashes curled tightly as he closed his eyes, and the look of bliss on his face was hard to dismiss. "Let me in," he breathed between the valley of her breasts as he plumped the mounds together and rubbed his stubbled cheek against her skin.

Elise let her legs fall open and D settled between them with ease. They fit together, the thick bulge of his erection pressed against her softer sex. She clutched at his head, tugging him closer, needing the sensations he pulled from her like a drug.

Her head whirled.

This overwhelming urgency thrummed inside her like a low electric pulse. A frantic compulsion to hold on to this experience, to hold on to *him* ran through her. And they still had on their underwear.

She arched her back and curled her legs around his hips, pressing her sex against his erection. "I need you closer." She rocked her hips up into his hardness.

"Baby, this won't last, I won't last if you keep doin' that." He groaned against her neck. "I'm trying to make this good for you."

"Get 'er done." Elise panted against his cheek. She needed him. She needed this.

He laughed.

Laughed! She was dying here and he was shaking with a deep belly laugh. He stopped what he was doing, propped his torso on his elbows, and cocked his head. Amusement bled from him, his mouth (which should be on her breasts) spread in a wide smile, his teeth blindingly white in his face.

The move shifted his lower body harder against her soft flesh. She was swollen and wet and needy and he was laughing. "Did you just…"

She was this bolder version of herself right now. Elise shoved the elastic band of his boxer briefs and palmed his amazing hard butt. "I need you. Now."

He brushed the damp strands of her hair from her face. "Well, far be it from me to deny a lady in need." D'Andre skimmed his palms over her. Deftly flicking her bra open, he bent his head to her bared breasts even as his other hand smoothly slid her panties down her thighs.

The silky soft cap of his cock branded her belly. Elise moaned.

Her sex clenched. She was out of her mind.

D rolled them over, lifting her above his body, then setting her on his thighs.

He reached over to the bedside table and yanked open the drawer, clawing desperately through the contents.

He panted. "No glove, no love."

Elise took in his body. His chest was so defined the muscles rippled as he clenched the condom package in a victorious fist. She ran her palms over his chest and down his stomach.

His underwear trapped his cock against his belly, the dark ruby head glistening with pre-cum as it strained toward his belly button. The happy trail of black hair created a halo around his groin as she pushed the boxers down his thighs. His cock jutted toward her like a divining rod. She curled her fingers around his pulsing cock and D's eyes glazed when she pumped him once, slowly.

He was hot, thick, huge in her hand. She sat on his thighs, his coarser hair rubbed beneath her bare legs, her bra hung off her shoulders.

D ripped the package open. Then he jackknifed to sitting and handed her the condom.

His palms clasped her shoulders and slipped her bra down her back. She shrugged it off as he lifted her breasts to his mouth.

Elise rolled the latex over his erection. A faint tremor of trepidation nudged her as she catalogued how big he was. Her hand trembled as she hesitated.

"You okay?"

"It's—" she paused, swallowed "—been a while and you're…big."

He bussed her nipples, one then the other. "I told you I needed to slow down. I don't want to hurt you."

"Good plan." Except she was dying for him to get inside her.

D skimmed his fingers along her belly. The sensitive skin contracted, then he slid his fingers into the nest of curls that protected her sex.

Elise moaned and tipped her head back.

He played with her, rubbing and caressing her clit, gently slicking her arousal over her, preparing her body for his. Until she couldn't stand it anymore. Her body was weeping for him, clenching with a primal need for D to fill her up.

"Please, D," she whispered.

"You ready?"

"Yes," she rasped out.

He lifted her up and slowly impaled her on his erection. The look on his face arrested her. A harsh lust sharpened his features and sent a visceral, erotic thrill through her.

He pierced her body. The mushroom head of his cock pushed inside slowly, parting her and filling her with slow progress. An empty part of her she didn't know existed was suddenly full. Sensations bombarded her—the girth of his cock, the clasp of his hands on her hips, his sleek skin beneath her palms, the heated look in his eyes.

She was tempted to close her eyes to absorb all the sensations.

To close out that the intensity, protect her heart from the promise in his gaze, Elise slammed down the last few inches in a sudden thrust and claimed him.

"Unh."

As if he knew that she'd outworn her confidence, that she'd tested the limits of her ability to take control, D rolled them so that he was above her. But he wasn't moving.

Move, move, move, she chanted silently.

The connection, like a line spun between them, linked them on a cerebral plane as well as physical.

He began to rock into her. Elise savored all the sensations—the salty taste of his skin on her tongue, the sweat as their bodies rocked together, his cockhead rubbing on the ridge of what she'd assumed was a mythical G-spot, her nipples scraping against his chest, his hips thrusting in the cradle of hers, the sure embrace of his arms around her. With every push, he hit various erogenous points, spiraling her higher. Her head was dizzy and her heart banged against her ribs so hard her breasts shimmied beneath him.

D held back, determination on his face, making it clear he wouldn't let go until she had come. They were wild, slamming together in an erotic frenzy.

Elise buried her face in his neck when he slid his hands beneath her ass and lifted her into his strokes. The shift in position hurtled her over the edge. She splintered apart into a million little pieces. Like fireworks bursting over the harbor, the reflected ripples floated across her consciousness as this beautiful man blew apart her world and shattered her expectations.

When D groaned into her ear and let go, his erection pulsed inside her, setting off more detonations in her body. His body stiffened and he arched back in a rictus of beauty. His muscles strained and his body contracted as he emptied into the condom.

Elise smoothed her palms over his shoulders and chest, soothing him with her touch as he collapsed into her embrace.

They lay there, her heart still galloping and her body buzzing with a contentment she hadn't expected. A sense of intimacy surrounded them in the dim light of his bedroom.

From the other room, her phone buzzed again in her purse.

Her father.

"Ignore it," D ordered.

"My father can be…difficult."

He shifted off her. "Don't want to crush you."

She'd wondered about his father. But now wasn't the time to ask.

"I can hear you thinking," he teased.

"You don't want to know."

"C'mon. Go for it."

"You never talk about your father." His relationship with his mother was so close.

"He's a nonentity."

She'd pulled his birth certificate while researching him. His father was listed as unknown. "Why?"

"Off the record? Because I don't let anything touch my mother."

She loved that he was all about protecting his mother. She should probably take offense but she knew how random comments could become the entire lynch pin for a story. "Off the record."

"He and my mother were just a hookup." His heartbeat slowed beneath her ear. His words were easy, not tense. "When she figured out she was pregnant, she tracked him down."

She waited, breath held.

"He couldn't handle having a baby. And she wasn't about to get an abortion." He shrugged.

Elise marveled at his sheer lack of feeling. "You seem… fine with that."

"I've had a long time to come to grips with the fact." He really wasn't holding on to the wound of a neglectful parent. "Intellectually, I understand, especially when you consider at first you can't see anything, you can't touch an embryo. It must have not seemed real. And they were very young."

But?

"But emotionally, I'm still angry for my momma." D trailed a finger along her pearls. "He basically left her to it. She deserved more. And now I try to give it to her."

She tried not to be pissed about the fact that his father had abdicated any personal responsibility but some of her anger must have come through. And she marveled that he didn't harbor any anger on his own behalf. "So, no father."

He rubbed his palm over her back, petting her like he'd soothe an animal. "I had other father figures in my life and they filled in when necessary. And my mother was a force to be reckoned with." She could feel his smile against her forehead.

"You are a really remarkable man." Elise pressed a soft kiss to his pectoral. "She done good."

She shouldn't have brought the interview into bed with them. But she wanted to know him. And when she'd asked it really hadn't been about an interview, it been about getting to know the man she'd just had sex with.

Of course, she shouldn't be *in* bed with him. And later she'd probably worry about what she'd just done, but for now she was going to live in the moment. And what the hell, they had already broken an unwritten rule. "On the record now."

"Seriously? You gonna interview me while we're both naked?"

"It's an easy one, hopefully. Who's your hero? Who do you look up to?"

No hesitation. "Michael Jordan."

"Why do you admire him?"

"First sports celebrity to hit billionaire status."

"And?" She knew there was more than that. For all his supposed talk of becoming a billionaire, he didn't seem to care that much about money. He seemed to always be giving it away.

"He was also the first Black athlete to really translate his brand beyond his sport."

But she wanted more. What was D's connection to Michael Jordan? "So that's it, brand and your heritage in common? Nothing else?"

"He was the best at his chosen profession. He excelled at basketball, always striving for the next level, not just in sports but in life."

It sounded like D had tried to model his own life after those principles.

"I remember a quote from an article written by Coach Jackson, and he said, Jordan's defining characteristic wasn't his talent, but having the humility to know he had to work constantly to be the best." His muscles were tense, almost as if he expected her to laugh. He swallowed. "So that's what I do. I strive to be the best."

Elise rested her head on his shoulder, giving him a moment to scoop up all those emotions and tuck them away again so he could be the big, tough football player.

"Lightning round."

"Again…while we're naked?"

"It's a new journalism technique." She giggled.

"Hit me."

"Cake or ice cream?"

"Ice cream."

"Night owl or early riser?"

"Early riser, but I can be persuaded to be a night owl if the incentive is right."

"What's the right incentive?"

"I can show you…" He rolled so that she was beneath him again and kissed his way down her belly, pausing at the top of her mound. "Off the record."

Chapter Twelve

D didn't usually have women stay over.

Typically ever. The only reason he could come up with for the aberration in his MO was that last night had been abnormal in almost every way possible.

It had been a night of nevers.

But he thought that when he did have someone stay over they would want to actually relax. So it was kind of a surprise when he woke to find Elise hastily yanking on her lace panties.

He was wrecked. They'd had sex again and she'd fallen asleep on top of him. He hadn't gotten that itch to move, to extricate from her arms. Instead, he'd held her close, and after some contortions to get the condom off with a little leakage, he'd pulled her close and savored the weight of her on top of him.

Her corn-silk hair had stuck to his neck, and her breasts pillowed against his pecs as she snuffled in his ear. She didn't snore exactly but a small chuff of breath against his skin tickled him.

"Give me a sec." He had a sex hangover. He shoved to

sitting and pressed his elbows on his knees and rubbed the heel of his hands on his eyeballs.

"What time is it?" she shrieked, hopping on one foot as she tried to pull on one of her pumps.

Ah, those pumps.

He patted his palm over his heart. "You are hot AF."

"What?" She stood, all sleek long legs and ivory lace and shiny heels. Her pearls were still wrapped around her neck. Jesus she was like a prim and proper fantasy girl.

"Focus, D'Andre."

Even her snippy tone was turning him on. D glanced at the clock. It was only five-thirty.

"It's early."

"Not early enough. I have to get home." She stomped out to the living room and he followed. Buck naked. A full body flush started at her stomach and spread, pinkening her breasts and coloring her neck and face.

She was tugging her clothes on.

And then she froze.

Stood. Blushed even harder. "Oh dear Lord. How could I forget?" She slapped her palm to her forehead. "I need a ride."

He hadn't forgotten. "I know. Let me pull on some sweats and I'll take you."

"You don't have to. If I could borrow a few dollars…."

Her attitude was becoming less funny. Was she ashamed of last night? He sure wasn't. Although sleeping with her wasn't advisable, it wasn't the end of the world.

He gave her a look. On the football field, defensive linemen cowered beneath that glare. "I'll take you."

"Okay." She straightened her dress. "Thank you," she said softly.

Elise turned around and faced the dark morning of the

Boston skyline while D got dressed. "It's so minimalist," she said glancing around his apartment. The clean lines and sleek furniture gave an impression of wide open space. "Of course, my house is filled with generations of furniture and the weight of expectations."

She frowned. And when she didn't say anything else, he thought maybe he'd misunderstood her comments about her family home. Because now he got the impression she disapproved of his space.

"I didn't grow up with a lot of stuff, junk." *Dirt poor* would be the words for it. But she already knew that.

She didn't say anything else. Just tilted her head, her straight platinum hair brushing her bare shoulders.

"I don't need things to feel complete." His life was full, overflowing with abundance.

"Which is admirable. Things won't make you happy," she countered.

Okay so she didn't disapprove of his space. Although why it bothered him, he'd have to explore later.

"But where do you keep all your books?" she murmured.

Ice froze his heart, and a peculiar fear overtook him. This was why he shouldn't have slept with her. Never mind that she made him laugh, challenged him, had a hidden level of compassion that he hadn't seen coming. She was dangerous to the life he'd built, one catch, one touchdown at a time.

"I have a Kindle," he said stiffly.

"Lightning round."

He already knew he didn't like where this was going. "We'll see."

"Classics or new bestseller?"

"Neither. Nonfiction." His sanity returned. "I'd best get you home."

Her lush mouth was pressed into a flat line. "Good idea."

"Can't let you take that walk of shame alone." D laughed. "Takes two."

❧

Walk of shame?

Elise pivoted around to face him. She thought about last night, that sense of intimacy, those moments of absolute bliss. "There's no shame in last night."

He lost the laugh. "True."

She cleared her throat. "No shame in taking control of your sexuality or sharing your body."

"Absolutely."

They totally agreed but the air was tense, at odds with their agreement.

"Didn't mean to offend you." He had the grace to look a bit embarrassed.

The walk of shame shouldn't be a thing. But the fact that he mentioned it made her wonder.

How many women had he driven home in the early morning? Of course since he'd taken offense at the book question, he definitely wouldn't answer that one.

"What?"

"What, what?"

"You had a look on your face."

Fine. She'd ask. "Off the record."

He nodded slowly.

"I was wondering how many hundreds of women you've driven home in the morning."

He propped his hands on his hips. The branded

sweatpants hung low, and the tight muscle tank sculpted to every pec and trap and ab like a lover.

She'd kissed every one of those muscles last night, and her knees went weak when she thought about his strength and his tenderness.

"You really want to know?"

She braced for the number, knowing she would hate to be one of the masses. Nodded.

"One."

One?

"A hundred?" Her voice rose. She couldn't help it. Thank God they'd used condoms.

He huffed out a disgruntled breath. "Jesus, woman. Not one hundred."

That meant…one?

Elise blinked. She thought about Stacey Jackson in the bathroom and how she'd been frustrated that she hadn't gotten him in bed.

D crowded in on her, used his index finger to push her chin up and close her mouth. He leaned closer and breathed in her ear. "One."

"But…you're D'Andre Smith."

"I know who I am."

He did. He was supremely confident in who he was. She admired how comfortable he was in his own skin.

"Groupies lost their appeal after my rookie year."

Okay. But still. She was trying to process his response.

"I was raised by a single mother. I would never put a woman through what my mother went through. She taught me to be smart about women. About sex."

Now Elise blushed. Which was stupid. She'd had sex with him. Twice.

But somehow the frank discussion with all their clothes on was far more intimate than being naked.

Their conversation had gotten extremely personal. Extremely quickly.

"I don't fuck around. And I don't want to be some woman's trophy fuck," D said. "I'm extremely discriminating."

Elise hesitated. "Neither do I."

He was silent.

"Sleep with groupies." She couldn't help but push.

His face was a blank mask but then he grinned. "Good to know."

That sense of triumph at getting him to laugh was weird.

D flipped his keys around his finger. "Where to?"

Oh, ugh. Now she had to sneak into her family home because while she had nothing to be ashamed of…her father definitely wouldn't see it that way.

❧

ELISE SCAMPERED in through the front door.

D's Escalade was already down the street and about to turn the corner. Her father was typically up early but hopefully he hadn't emerged from his suite of rooms yet.

She held the ornate knob tightly, pressing the door closed with a gentle click.

She'd managed to keep her freak-out hidden from D'Andre while he drove her home. She'd slept with him. There was so much she needed to unpack from last night. But first she needed a shower and a cup of coffee.

Elise sighed, dropped her shoulders, and turned.

"Where have you been?"

She jumped.

Shock, surprise—her heart thudded at the menace in his voice.

Elise lifted her chin. "Out."

Her father grimaced in disgust. "Well, I know you weren't out with your date, his father called me last night. How dare you embarrass him?"

She embarrassed *him*?

"He was drunk," Elise said flatly. "We saved him from the legal problems of a DUI, not to mention from possibly harming someone."

"*We?*" Her father radiated disapproval.

Elise headed for the stairs. Her relationship with her father was fraught to say the least, and she wasn't about to discuss this with him.

He shook the newspaper at her. Temper shone red and high on his cheekbones, and his cold eyes glittered with something she didn't like. "Our whole world can guess who you went home with."

"What are you talking about?"

He slapped the folded newspaper against her shoulder.

Elise spread it open. The society page had two pictures from last night. The one of Elise and D'Andre dancing intimately, and the picture of her with Mary Smith and her son. Elise smiled. She liked his mother.

She was extremely admirable. And funny. And warm. And real.

"What are you smiling about?" he snarled. "This is an embarrassment."

"It's great press for his foundation and D'Andre Smith's company," Elise clipped out. "The foundation is for an admirable cause and the helmet is going to make a huge difference in the protection and diagnosis of concussions."

Her father pfft-ed. "I meant for us."

"You're the one who insisted I attend the fundraiser," Elise said mildly. She refused to rise to his obvious taunt.

"Attend. Not consort with athletes," Father snarled. "You were supposed to be forging a connection with Alexander Weld."

"He was offensive and drunk the entire evening."

Her father didn't say anything, practically rolling his eyes at her. Did he not care that Weld was a jerk?

"Fortunately D'Andre Smith has a moral compass, and made sure Alex got home without killing himself or anyone else."

"So what, now you…like him?"

"D?" She knew the familiarity would annoy her father and she did it anyway. "He's an upstanding pillar of the Boston community."

"He's not our kind."

"What does that even mean?" she demanded. But she was afraid she knew.

"You have a legendary bloodline to carry on." He sniffed. "He is hardly an appropriate candidate."

She wanted to challenge him. To call him out on his bigotry and racism but she didn't want to taint her memories of last night. D'Andre Smith had been an attentive and wonderful lover. He had literally rocked her world. And letting her father tarnish those moments seemed like the ultimate betrayal.

Before she could say anything that would prompt another argument, she pivoted toward the stairs.

"Wait." There was a note in her father's voice that had her turning around. But he just slapped a piece of paper in her hand. "You have a coffee date with another prospect this morning."

She needed to work on the profile about D'Andre. She had an appointment to speak with his high school coach. She wanted to lie in bed and savor last night before the day crashed in on her. But apparently she didn't have time because she had another date.

An out-of-control feeling overtook her. The urge to lash out at her father was strong but she tempered it and said calmly, "Father, I'm really not interested in getting married yet. I want to experience life before I start having children." Hoping, hoping that he would surely understand. He hadn't gotten married until he was thirty.

He stared at her, disapproval set his face into an unforgiving frown. "You will find a husband, or I will stop being interested in letting you live here."

❧

ELISE ARRIVED at Tatte Bakery early.

She grabbed a pistachio croissant and a latte but when she went to pay for her breakfast, her card was declined.

"Oh, that's not right. Let's try again. Maybe there's a computer glitch at my bank." But a sinking feeling in the pit of her stomach made her wonder if the issue was more worrisome. She had a ten-thousand-dollar limit on the card though she rarely spent more than a thousand a month, which her father paid.

Elise pushed the card in the reader again and punched in her pin.

After a few seconds, the machine blared a loud horn sound and the words *Denied* flashed on the screen. The girl behind the counter shifted her gaze to the cash register and shook her head. "Nope."

Elise flushed and dug through the sports belt at her hips

that held a small notebook, pen, credit card and cash, scrounging up a ten to cover the cost.

She sat at a table outside to enjoy the cool early morning. Her stomach cramped when she realized that her father intended to basically hold her hostage to his demands. She'd already blown through her meager paycheck and didn't get paid again until next Friday. She needed to watch her expenses so she could save enough money to move out.

The day promised to be a scorcher. In defiance, she'd worn workout gear and run to the popular eatery, treating the meet casual rather than like a date.

She had several satellite interviews set up with the sources D'Andre had agreed to let her speak to. After his high school coach, she needed to talk with Jay Hollingsworth. She needed to be prepared. She was jotting down potential interview questions when a shadow fell over her.

"Elise?" The perfectly coiffed man was dressed like a preppy bomb had detonated all over him. Plaid, pink, Vineyard Vines, and Sperry's. He had more hairspray in his hair than she'd worn last night.

She nodded mutely.

"Neil." He thrust out his smooth, soft manicured hand and shook. But for all he was pampered, his grip was solid. "I see you started without me."

She shrugged, feeling a bit of shame. It wasn't Neil's fault that she'd been pissed at her father, at the situation. "My apologies."

"It's fine, darling." He dragged out an iron bistro chair and plopped into the seat.

Darling? Elise eyed Neil again. No way was he interested in her.

He nipped a bite of her croissant and closed his eyes in

bliss. "That is di-vine." He crossed his legs and propped his elbow, chin on his fist, on the small table. "So."

Elise was at a loss.

"You looked fabulous in that lace dress." He smirked.

Elise blinked. "You were there?"

"Ah, no," Neil said. "Saw you while doing my morning perusal of Instagram."

"Instagram?" She hadn't posted anything.

"The delectable Mr. Smith dancing with you was snapped and posted multiple times. You were lost in each other. Plenty of weeping by his adoring fans."

"It was a *dance*." Nothing more.

But Neil wasn't even listening to her. He tapped a manicured finger on his mouth. "He really should have capitalized on the exposure. He should be using a standard hashtag and pushing to all his social media outlets."

"What are you talking about?"

"Publicity, darling. I'm in PR."

Well, that made sense.

"One assumes that the extremely hot football player in the pictures was not your date."

Elise flushed, cleared her throat. "No."

"Bet your daddy had a kitten."

Elise snorted, trying to hold back her laugh. "That's an understatement."

"So if you weren't there with D'Andre, who was your suitor?"

She named her date.

"Oh, dear. Stay away from that one." Neil shook his head. "Rumor is he's got quite the temper."

He asked her about the others on her list. Elise studied him for a moment, then decided what the hell? And told him.

He gossiped about each of them, which normally she wouldn't condone, but she'd been out of the social scene for the past few years.

"Um, what about you?"

"Me?"

"Why are you, um…" She didn't want to offend him but there was no way he played for her team.

"Heirs, darling." He sighed, his shoulders slumping slightly.

"You just want someone to pop out a few kids?" she couldn't help but ask.

"That about sums it up," Neil said. "I was hopeful that since you were willing to meet that perhaps…."

"No." Elise didn't know what else to say. "I'm sorry."

"Me too. I really want to get this over with so I can get on with my life. And so my boyfriend doesn't leave me."

She fought the need to apologize. Her gaze skittered to the traffic on Beacon and she straightened her shoulders. "Why can't you just adopt?"

But of course that was naïve. For the same reason her father wanted her to join with the right bloodlines.

"One must procreate," Neil intoned.

"Our fathers must have worked on that speech together," she said glumly. What the hell was she going to do? She'd have to keep going on dates until she could figure out a new place to live.

He pulled another piece of croissant from her plate.

"So dish about D'Andre." Neil raised a groomed eyebrow and gave her a sly look.

Elise flushed.

"Oh my God, you slept with him." Neil clapped like he'd just heard the best news.

"Shut up." Elise slapped at his fingers. "What is wrong with you?"

"Please, please, please tell me he's as good in bed as he was in the end zone." He flapped his hand as if he was overheated. "That man has moves."

"He's…a really nice guy."

"You like him." Neil sighed.

Elise froze.

She did like him.

Oh that would never do. She was supposed to be writing a profile about him. In a fit of anger regarding her father, she'd broken a cardinal rule of journalism and slept with her subject.

The opportunity to show her boss that she was capable of more than copy editing was her ticket out of this miserable situation. Her father had threatened to kick her out. The threat hadn't even been that subtle.

And apparently he'd cut off her access to money.

That quickly, she was glum all over again.

"You sure you don't want to bear my children and then we can go our separate ways?" Neil grinned.

"No."

"Hmm, but in the meantime, what about a deal?"

❧

SATURDAY MORNINGS WERE RESERVED for breakfast with his momma. But today all she wanted to talk about was Elise. The reporter he'd slept with. Before Elise had even entered her house after he'd dropped her off, he'd been second-guessing last night.

"What's going on with you and Elise Putnam?" She waved a newspaper at him.

D grabbed the paper and stared at the pictures from the fundraiser. For a second, he panicked. What if she'd been identified as a reporter on the social page? But when he slowly read through the caption, they merely mentioned their names, identifying her as a socialite, and the name of his company and the IMPACT'D foundation. Thank fuck.

"I like her."

"She's…white," he said cautiously.

"Not what I expected, that's for sure." A serene smile wreathed her face. "But I'm wanting to see you settled."

D opened his mouth. Closed it. "What?"

Okay, that was a surprise. And the fact that his mother mentioned *settled* and *Elise* in the same conversation shocked the hell out of him.

"She's got class. Why wasn't she with you last night? And what were you doing with the hussy you were dancing with?"

"Stacey is not a hussy, she's just very…comfortable with her body."

"And she's got a good one, but we weren't at no disco. That was serious business."

D was still hung up on the fact that his mother liked Elise.

"You planning on seeing her again?"

"Stacey?" He deliberately misunderstood.

"D. Andre. Walter. Smith." Momma cocked her head, her ringlets jiggling as she narrowed her eyes at him.

D squirmed. This was the perfect time to tell his mother that Elise was a reporter. But he just couldn't do it. "Yeah, she's going to volunteer with me at the Boys & Girls Club this afternoon."

"I told you I liked her."

He didn't want his mother to like her. He wanted his mother to stay out of his life.

D shoveled more eggs into his mouth. "These are great, Momma."

"You aren't gettin' around this subject so fast." Momma poured more coffee into his mug. "Dorothea's friend Franny works for that family."

D continued to eat, not giving his mother any more fuel.

"Apparently her daddy is a right bastard. But Franny says that Miss Elise is a doll baby. She took care of her mother for over two years."

D nodded and slurped his coffee. "I know."

"Listen to your momma. Don't let this girl go."

But he didn't have her. Not really, and when his mother found out that Elise was a reporter, there would be hell to pay.

Chapter Thirteen

❧

Elise got off the T and headed for the Boys & Girls Club.

She'd promised D that she'd help at today's event. They'd agreed that this was meeting number two. Number one had been half weight lifting and half running. She'd come with a mental list of questions, but she wondered how much time they would really get to spend together. At least she could observe him in a more public setting.

After she got home from breakfast, she'd checked her bank account and discovered that her card was frozen. Her father had apparently decided to force her hand.

She and Neil had come up with a temporary solution to both their problems and were going to "date" for a few weeks. So later, she would try to reason with her father.

If he refused to back down on cutting off her credit card, she could get access to some money from her trust, but she couldn't get a request processed until Monday.

Fortunately, she had enough cash to get to and from today's location. A giant banner slung across the entrance said, "Welcome D'Andre Smith!"

A line of parents and kids stretched around two corners of the block, the excitement in the air palpable. She studied the line of waiting kids. She couldn't cut in front of all these people.

I'm here to pay up. She texted him. *How do I get in?*

He replied almost immediately. *Come around the back.*

A spurt of trepidation hit her low in the solar plexus at seeing him again. But even stronger than that hesitation was the jittery feeling in her belly. Their intimacy couldn't happen again and that was a crying shame.

D opened the back door of the facility, his broad shoulders filling the doorway, and let her in. He was in designer jeans and a purple Boys & Girls Club T-shirt. "Thanks for coming."

"I would never renege on a promise." She grinned. "The crowd is super excited."

He led her into a large gymnasium with basketball hoops at both ends, bleachers and a line of folding tables decorated with balloons and metallic streamers. The tables were jam-packed with row upon row of stuffed backpacks while others held sleeping bags.

"What's today's mission?" Elise asked.

"The backpacks are filled with camping supplies so these kids can attend overnight camp in the mountains."

"What a lovely idea," Elise said wistfully.

"Right? Sleeping outside in tents, hiking, s'mores."

She'd gone to plenty of summer camps—basketball, tennis, sailing—when she was a kid and they'd been a blast, but she'd never spent a night in a sleeping bag exploring the outdoors. "I've never been camping."

D laughed. "Me either. But it always sounded like fun."

A slightly harried woman fluttered around D. "We're

almost ready to let the kids in. Do you have everything you need?"

"Juanita, this is Elise. Juanita is an angel."

The Hispanic woman blushed. "Pretty sure you're our angel, Mr. Smith."

He took her hand gently and held on. "Thank you for taking care of all the details." He squeezed the woman's hand and Elise thought the woman might faint. She was definitely starstruck. And D took his time, calming her down and setting her at ease.

Once she was settled, Elise and D had a moment alone.

"What do you want me to do?"

"My assistant had a commitment so if you can fill in for him that would be great. Just keep me stocked with pictures, sharpies, and a bottle of water."

"I'm basically Santa's elf."

"You can sit on my lap any time." The suggestion in his voice sent a tingle through her girl parts.

He handed her an oversized T and she slipped it over her head and knotted the extra length on one hip.

The gym was set up so that the kids could get their backpack and sleeping bag and then get an autograph from D. They had him at a table and as the kids and parents started filing in, the screeches when they saw him were adorable. D ducked his head for a second then lifted his chin and smiled at the incoming participants.

Elise stood behind D's left shoulder. "You seem embarrassed."

"This is a great cause," he said diplomatically.

"But?"

"I prefer more hands-on events, but if I try to volunteer, the focus isn't on the actual event but on me."

The first kid made his way to D's table. The next few

hours were chaotic and loud and enlightening. He made the effort to speak to every kid and parent.

One quiet, soft-spoken boy, about eleven, maybe twelve, had a very solemn expression on his face as he asked for an autograph. With his dark skin and curly black hair he probably looked similar to D at the same age. His mother was tall, slender, with an Afro crown of hair, tilted eyes brightened with shimmering gold shadow, and a wide full mouth slicked with bronze gloss.

Just the kind of woman that usually accompanied D'Andre Smith to his social functions. Beside her Elise felt like a pale wraith.

D smiled at the kid *and* his mother.

"Thanks, D." But the kid didn't look happy—if anything, after getting his autograph he looked dejected. Only the top of his curly hair was visible as he stared down at D's autographed picture.

"What's wrong, my man?"

The kid swallowed. "I really like football."

"Me too."

"My coach says I'm really good." His mother behind him wore a strained smile on her gorgeous face.

"That's great."

The kid's mouth turned down and he shook his head. "I have trouble in school."

D stiffened. If Elise hadn't been expressly watching she probably would have missed his reaction. "If you work hard, you can do it."

The kid replied, "Sure." But it was clear he didn't believe D's statement.

"What's your name, kid?"

The kid's response was so soft, D had to lean forward. He put his massive hand on the boy's shoulder. "Keep up the good work." But he held up his finger, in the classic sign to wait, and gestured to Elise.

She leaned over and he whispered in her ear. "Can you get this boy's name and his mom's cell number? Do it under the guise of taking a photo of us and sharing it with them."

That sick feeling in the pit of her stomach intensified. He wanted the woman's phone number.

"Absolutely." Elise's smile wanted to tug down at the corners as she spoke to the pair. "Come over and stand behind Mr. Smith, and I'll get your picture."

The mother's eyes widened and Elise positioned them behind D. After snapping a few pics, she moved the family over to the bleachers so that the line could keep moving. She spoke to the mom, "Can I get your name and cell phone number?"

"What for?"

Elise didn't know for sure. It was possible that D had some altruistic motive in mind, but it was also possible that he was using Elise to set up his next conquest.

"So that I can send you the picture." She held up D's smart phone."

"D'Andre Smith is okay with me having his number?" the mom said, clearly suspicious and hopeful at the same time.

"It's so I can send the photo. Is that okay?"

"Yes!" The kid jumped up and down. "Please, Mom."

The mother agreed and Elise forwarded the best one and tried not to let jealousy overtake her. The burn beneath her breastbone told her she hadn't quite succeeded. But she needed to let it go.

As they walked away, Elise glanced at D's phone and saw the Instagram app.

"You want me to post a pic of you on Instagram?"

For a second, he looked uncomfortable. "I guess so. Usually my assistant takes care of my social media."

Elise snapped a few of D at his table, then uploaded the best photo and added some hashtags that would call attention to the Boys & Girls Club and this fundraiser in particular.

"You don't post your own?" She'd leaned closer.

"Why the hell does anyone care what my breakfast looks like?" he growled.

"You're a public figure."

"Still. Some things oughtta be private."

His disgruntled expression made her giggle. "I finally found a flaw."

"What are you talking about? I'm perfect."

Another kid approached the table and D morphed back into the consummate professional. His smile warm and his attention genuine, he really was perfect.

Much later, after all the kids were gone, D stayed another few hours and interacted with the staff and volunteers of the club.

Juanita came up to Elise as she was gathering up the final photos D had autographed and left for those kids who weren't attending camp or who couldn't come today. "Thank you for your help today."

"I was happy to do it." Elise smiled. "How often does he do this kind of thing?"

"More than you'd think. He's incredibly generous with his time…and other things." Juanita stacked chairs as she and Elise chatted.

Elise subtly pressed Juanita for information. She wouldn't be able to use specifics in the article but any background she could pick up on D would be useful.

Juanita asked, "How long have you two been…"

"Friends?"

"If that's what we're calling it these days." Her smile was sly.

Elise flushed. "We really are just friends."

D came up next to Elise and slung his arm around her shoulders. His touch was gentle, proprietary, and she couldn't help the little thrill that ran through her.

"I took some pictures on my phone," Juanita said. "I'm fixing to post them on the website if that's okay with you."

"Of course." D glanced around the now empty gym. "Thank you again for putting this together."

Elise's heart sank and she was caught between pride and irritation. Hopefully the pictures would stay just on the website and not be posted anywhere else. She didn't want her father to see more pictures of her with D, and yet bringing awareness to a fabulous cause was important. Her troubles seemed petty compared with the kids who'd come today.

"If you're done with me, I'm going to take off." Elise peered out the window at the dusk sky. It must be later than she'd thought. She checked her watch, surprised at how much time had passed. "I had no idea how late it was."

D said, "Let me drive you home. We far exceeded the two hours you were supposed to be here."

"Juanita, it was a pleasure to meet you." Elise held out her hand.

"Likewise." Juanita eyed D's arm which was still possessively wrapped around her shoulders.

"Let's go."

"I appreciate the ride. I'm not all that familiar with the T schedule and wasn't sure how often it runs at night."

D shot her a quizzical look. "You took the T?"

"There's nothing wrong with public transportation."

"Of course not. I'm just surprised that you avail yourself of the fabulous system we enjoy in Boston."

She wasn't about to admit that until recently, she rarely taken the train. But cabs were no longer a luxury she could afford.

They hopped in his Escalade and he pulled onto the street. This time of night on a Saturday, the streets were crowded, cars and taxis zipping in and out of traffic as he headed toward downtown.

The silence in his truck went on a little too long.

Elise's stomach growled in the somewhat tense air. That pistachio croissant had been a long time ago. The club had served sandwiches but neither Elise or D had eaten any.

"You want to grab some dinner?"

She thought about going home to her empty mausoleum. Franny would be retired for the night and Elise wouldn't want to bother her. But as for going out, she didn't have enough money.

"It's okay. You can take me home."

D's stomach grumbled. "That wasn't an answer, and I'm starving."

"Okay, well then we can stop so you can get food, and I'll eat when I get home."

"Suddenly, I'm not good enough to eat with?" he jabbed.

Elise shot back, "I don't have any money for food." She crossed her arms over her stomach. Shame cascaded through her.

D stopped at a light, turned to study her. Elise shifted her gaze out the window. "I think I can afford dinner to spring for your dinner," he said drily.

"Okay." The word rasped in her throat. She swallowed. "Thanks."

"Don't mention it."

Silently they drove through the streets. The wail of a fire engine siren and the honking horns were the only noise in the quiet car.

Elise blinked when she realized they were at the entrance to D's garage. "What are we doing here?"

"Hope you don't mind but if I go out in public, I'll be mobbed. And after today, I need a little peace." D pulled into his parking spot and turned off the engine.

"You were really good with the kids." He had impressed her with his kindness and patience. Her heart softened. "Of course. It's fine. You're probably tired. I can just catch the T home from here."

"Elise, you aren't the public, and I'll drive you home."

"Okay. How did you survive the constant press on your time when you were playing?" she asked curiously. The question was one she didn't get to ask before. "I have a list of questions I didn't get to today."

"I guess I owe you since we didn't have time to…talk at the event."

He really did.

Chapter Fourteen

❧

D WANTED TO DESTROY THE MELANCHOLY AURA THAT surrounded Elise.

She'd been a trooper helping him out all day.

Why the fuck was little miss heiress taking the T? And what was up with her not having money for dinner?

"Capital Grille good for you?" He unlocked the door to his condo and gestured for her to go inside.

The oversized Boys & Girls Club T covered her butt and only hinted at her breasts. The urge to strip the purple cotton from her and explore that lithe, responsive body thrummed below the surface. But he wasn't an animal.

"Oh, I don't need anything fancy."

D flopped on the sofa and spread his long legs out. Elise sat down across from him, very prim and proper. And shit, the need to muss her up was like a compulsion.

He better focus on something he could take care of. Like his hunger. "I'm in the mood for a steak and their mashed potatoes are godlike."

"Um, okay."

"What kind of steak you want?"

"Whatever's cheapest." She waved away her wants with a flick of those pink-tipped nails.

He pulled out his cell and pressed a single button. "Hey." D went through the obligatory chitchat. He was truly thankful that he could get an order delivered without much fuss. "Prime rib, medium rare, béarnaise and that red wine sauce, a filet—" he placed his hand over the mouthpiece "—How do you like yours cooked?"

"Medium. But you don't have to—"

"Medium. Just give us a complement of all your sauces. Plus mashed potatoes, a double order on those, asparagus—you got those Brussel sprouts with the candied bacon?—maybe some creamed spinach, plus two Caesar salads."

They recited the order back to him.

"Yeah, put it on my tab. And any kind of rush you could put on that would be awesome." D hung up.

Elise's ice-blue eyes warmed and widened. "How many people are you feeding?" she teased.

"I have needs." D rubbed his belly. While her T-shirt was overly large, his fit snugly. And her eyes lingered on his hand.

And just like that the room heated again. Those forbidden thoughts swirled through his mind, and his body reacted predictably.

"Thanks for putting in the extra time today."

That awkwardness between them was back. D wasn't sure what he'd done but he hated this.

"It was no problem." She sat stiffly in one of the side chairs. "What are you planning to do with that mother's phone number?"

D shifted. He didn't know. He wanted to help. "Not sure."

She rolled her eyes. "If you don't want to tell me, that's

fine." Then, as if she couldn't help herself, she blurted out, "She was gorgeous."

"That's *not* why I wanted her number."

Elise grunted.

"Jesus, I can get my own dates, thank you very much."

"Well, maybe not since you're ordering takeout with me on a Saturday night," she shot back.

D started. "Maybe I want this to be a date."

That shut her up.

Of course, it shut him up too. Before he could press her further, the doorbell buzzed. Food was there. Thank the Lord. Because dating the woman who was supposed to be interviewing him, a reporter for Lord's sake, was the height of stupid, and contrary to the past few minutes he wasn't a dumbass.

They both had barriers to changing this relationship. Which was for the best, even if it didn't really feel like it.

D brought the giant takeout bag into the kitchen. "Grab silverware and napkins from the drawer next to the dishwasher." He avoided looking at her as he lay out the feast.

And she studiously avoided looking at him, so great, they both didn't know how to move on from his ill-advised and ill-thought-out wish.

When they sat down at the sleek black table, she placed the phone between them, which doused his ardor faster than a mandatory stay on the injured reserve list.

That phone sat between them, the elephant in the room, reminding her of her responsibilities and reminding him of the fact that his mother hated reporters and he wasn't far behind.

Elise received a text. She looked at the message and then sent a quick reply.

"Who was that?"

"Our housekeeper just wondering about my ETA. I forgot to let her know I wasn't coming home for dinner."

Her phone kept pinging. She picked it up and smiled. "Hey, that Instagram pic is getting lots of love."

D shrugged. He really didn't care. He didn't understand the obsession to know everything about public figures. Needing to know everything was how people were disappointed.

"I added some hashtags you should consider putting on every post." She had a silly little smile on her face as she canted her head and sent a quick text. "My date this morning gave me some pointers for you."

"Another date?"

And that quickly her smile disappeared.

"Yes." Elise concentrated on slicing her steak.

"What's up with that?"

She blinked. Didn't answer.

"Come on. You want me to bare my life to you for an article." D had stopped eating. "Throw me a bone."

He'd like to throw her a bone.

Nope, D. Not a good idea.

"My father wants me to get married and pop out some babies."

"And you can't say no?" Because that didn't seem right.

"Right now I don't make enough to support myself." Elise shook her head. "But if I can prove to my boss that I can write, that I can produce quality articles, then the pay raise will be enough to live on my own so I'm not dependent on my father."

"He's…holding your ovaries hostage?"

She flushed. "That's one way of putting it," she muttered.

"So you really need this interview?"

"Yes."

D's earlier reluctance dissolved. They could help each other. She could give him the promo he wanted for his new company and he could help her with her job.

He still hated the idea of an interview, but now that he understood, he liked the idea of being able to help her out.

D plopped a giant scoop of mashed potatoes on his plate. "Okay. Hit me."

"Really?" And shit, her smile made him feel ten feet tall.

"Yeah." D shook his head, hoped he wouldn't regret this. "But be gentle with me."

She flushed again. "Thank you."

Hell, he knew how it felt to be powerless. The fact that he could help her out gave him a good feeling.

"How did you survive the constant press on your time?"

"I knew it was temporary. And it was what I worked for. Every time I had the urge to bail I remembered that people craved what I had and that I wanted to play pro ball. When you get to that level it isn't just about the love of the game anymore. I just had to make peace with that."

She jotted notes in her notebook and nodded. "You still get recognized when you're out in public. How do you balance that with a private life?"

"I guard my privacy pretty tightly." D ate slowly, enjoying the steak and oddly even her questions. "My inner circle is small and dedicated. I have a healthy publicity schedule and I stick to it. And I make sure to schedule down time."

"What were you supposed to do tonight then?"

"Dinner alone."

"You want me to get out of your hair?"

"I told you earlier. You aren't the public." And he

realized then that she wasn't. He was comfortable with her. Eminently so.

"A lot of players who come into the league end up broke several years after they leave the NFL. How did you avoid that?"

"I was lucky." D smiled. "My friends from the BBC had a lot more investment experience. I learned from them about how to invest and they were a good sounding board."

Elise folded her arms on the tabletop and leaned forward, listening intently.

"Also, my momma lived on a budget for years. She cautioned me about going crazy. I took everyone's advice and then I made a plan on how to avoid overspending."

Elise nodded. "What's your advice to new kids coming into the league?"

"Don't blow all your money the first year. It's tempting. A lot of guys come into the NFL making more money than they can even conceive of. I run a seminar for rookies to help them manage their money. I also invested in a startup that helps these young guys learn financial responsibility and invest wisely. I can't make them save their money but if I can help them avoid costly mistakes then I'm good."

Elise scribbled in the notebook. "You had to quit suddenly. Do you use your own situation as an example?"

"There are a hundred eager kids just longing for a shot at the big game and waiting for someone to get injured. I try to impress upon them that the only person who is gonna take care of them is them. The league chews up and spits out players without compunction. To them it's a business, to these kids it's their whole life."

"You like helping people." It wasn't a question.

"Yeah." D felt the compliment deep in his gut. He was a fixer. "I like knowing I've made a difference."

"That's…really nice."

"Kiss of death, y'all. Nice."

She laughed as he knew she would and he successfully distracted her.

D got up from the table and started clearing the dishes.

"So the BBC is still really important in your life." Elise stopped writing and closed her notebook. "I love that."

"Yeah. They're my best friends." As a matter of fact, tomorrow was their quarterly breakfast.

Elise stood from the table and brought dishes over to the sink. They worked in tandem, D scraped and rinsed the dish then Elise put it in the dishwasher.

"I still need to interview Jay. We've been going back and forth about times."

"You want to meet them?" The more he thought about it, the more he liked the idea.

"Them?"

"The BBC."

"Oh, I would love to, but—"

"We still meet for breakfast quarterly. And tomorrow is the day."

"They might not want me there." But he could hear the excitement in her voice.

"I'll check in with them, see if they're okay with it." D snapped his fingers. "Maybe you can do a feature on the whole group." It could be another source of income for her.

"That would be…amazing."

She stared at him in wonder, and the naked emotion on her face made him squirm. His brain flashed back to last night, the sheer bliss when she'd climaxed. He wanted that again.

The silence in the kitchen lengthened, stretched between

them, heavy with regret, because they both knew that having sex again wasn't happening.

A sense of loss filled him. He liked her. A lot.

A thick anticipation hovered in the air. D realized they'd both leaned in, their bodies aligned perfectly.

His eyes drifted shut.

"Lightning round," she burst out, stepping back.

D nodded, covering his disappointment. "Go."

"Steak or chicken."

"Chicken, except for my cheat day, which just happens to be today."

"Casual or Formal?"

"Exercise gear all the way, although I do have a soft spot for a woman in a tight dress and high heels."

Elise blushed.

That awareness that they'd both tried to ignore flared to life again.

Her lashes arced down to hide her gaze from him. D needed to see her eyes. He curled his fingers under her chin and lifted her head up.

"But you know, lately I'm just as partial to shapeless purple T-shirts and cropped jeans."

She stared into his eyes, her pupils dilated. The air in the kitchen heated and slowed. D wanted to spend hours exploring her, making go soft and hazy with lust.

She exhaled in a puff of breath, and swayed toward him.

"This is a really bad idea." But even as she spoke, her lips brushed his.

"A terrible, no good, awful idea." D rested his hands on her hips and tugged her closer to his body. He slanted his head and dove into their kiss.

He might have stopped, except she kissed him like it was the best idea he'd ever had.

Elise curled her arms around his waist and hung on, her breasts pressing against his pecs, her body melting against his. She opened sweetly, her tongue stroking into his mouth.

Everything disappeared when he tasted her, and he never wanted this to end. But it really was an awful idea.

As if Elise realized the same, she broke away from him.

But D knew he didn't want her to go home just yet. "You want dessert?" He was grasping at any excuse to get her to stay a little longer.

"Sure," she said breathlessly.

"How about ice cream sundaes?"

Ice cream on cheat day was his weakness.

"Sounds great."

"Grab bowls from the cabinet while I get the supplies."

She put large bowls—smart girl—on the counter. D put out vanilla, chocolate, mint chip, chocolate syrup, whipped cream, and some chopped walnuts on the counter. Then he grabbed the scoop from a drawer.

"Serious business, huh?" Her smile lit up her blue eyes. And yes, they were back on easier footing, no sexual tension in sight. He could do this.

He could have dessert with her and then take her home. No compromising of ethics for either of them.

Elise opened the container and awkwardly began scooping ice cream.

"Girl, you are doing this all wrong." He grabbed the bottle of chocolate syrup. "You got to layer the ingredients in your bowl."

She was smirking at him. "There's a wrong way to make a sundae?"

"Absolutely. First a nice base of syrup." D squeezed the bottle but nothing came out.

The syrup was stuck.

D shook the plastic bottle and turned it upside down. Squeezed again. But nothing happened.

He gave it another hard jerk and then squeezed again.

The bottle came unstuck in a burst, and chocolate syrup shot everywhere, splattering on her cheek, neck and lips and the front of the T-shirt.

Elise shrieked when the cold syrup hit her face. Then she started laughing. "Oh my God." She lifted a hand to her cheek and used her finger to clean up a large line of chocolate on her cheek. Then she licked her finger, swiping her tongue over the tip, sweeping up the chocolate and sucking it into her mouth. "Yum."

D groaned at the sensual act. "Jay-sus. Sorry." He tossed the bottle on the counter and grabbed a dishtowel. He tried to dab at the chocolate but she was laughing too hard. "You're a sticky mess."

Then he stopped and really looked at her. She had smears of chocolate all over her face.

And he started to laugh.

"This is funny to you?" She narrowed her gaze and propped her fists on her hips. But it was hard to take her seriously since she looked like she'd painted stripes on her cheek, just like his days on the turf with eye black under his eyes.

He wheezed out a laugh then closed his eyes to wipe at the tears leaking out the sides. Something cold hit his face.

What the what?

D opened his eyes. The chocolate bottle was pointed straight at his face and another spurt of liquid hit his chin. "You want to go there?"

Now she was laughing so hard that taking the bottle from her was ridiculously easy. D grabbed the bottle and squirted at her chest, painting a smiley face on the cushion of her breasts.

She shrieked again. "What are you doing?"

"Payback, baby."

She grabbed for the bottle but he held it above his head as he advanced on her. Elise rounded the large black granite island, trying to keep a gulf of space between them.

She bobbed and weaved. Unfortunately he tried to anticipate her move and was wrong. The next squirt of chocolate hit her hair.

Her eyes rounded as she froze.

"Shit. Sorry. Sorry." D tossed the bottle on the counter and grabbed the towel again.

Elise brought her fingers up to the glob of chocolate in her hair. She still had barely moved when D hustled to her. "Let me get you cleaned up."

"You want to help me get this off?" she asked calmly.

"Yeah, yeah."

"Great." She scooped the big blob out of her hair and before he could wipe her fingers off she slathered the syrup all over his chin and mouth. Then she laughed like a loon. "Thanks for the assist," she wheezed.

He'd kept his hands and mouth judiciously far away from her. But he was only human.

He grabbed her by the waist and lifted her onto the island. Then he stepped between her legs and proceeded to kiss the hell out of her.

He kissed the chocolate from her cheeks and nose until he got to her mouth. Rather than clean her up, the move had just spread the chocolate from his face to hers.

Within moments, Elise was pushing his shirt up, and he

returned the favor, tearing the shirt over her head. They devoured each other, kissing as if they'd been stranded on a desert island for the past twenty years.

They broke apart roughly.

"What are we doing?" Hadn't they agreed this was a no good, terrible bad idea?

She arched into him. Today her bra was a pale lavender. And D wondered if her panties matched.

"Well if you don't know then your sex education was lacking," she said tartly.

D licked a path down the center of her body, taking time to suck her nipple into his mouth and play. He nipped and soothed and suckled even as his hands shaped her legs and hips before skimming across her belly.

He unzipped her jeans and lifted her easily so he could slide her jeans down her legs. And hot damn, the lace covering her pussy was lavender too.

"Clearly, my learnin' about your body is just fine."

"We're in the kitchen."

"And we're cooking." He nipped at her hip bone and then slid his fingers beneath the elastic at her belly until he connected with the curls protecting her sex.

"D," she said faintly. So much longing in that one syllable.

He tugged her panties off. She was spread out on his island, completely naked. Her cheeks were flushed, and here and there splotches of chocolate still decorated her face.

She gasped when he smiled against her thighs and then spread them wide with his shoulders.

"What are you doing?" She tugged at his hair. "Really, you don't have to—"

"Now look whose education is lacking?" He grinned, his mouth wide and smiling as he lapped at her. "This is never a 'have to' situation but a 'how many times can I get to.'"

Elise threw back her head as he tickled and teased and taunted her with his tongue. Her skin flushed and her thighs trembled as he took her to new heights.

And as she crested and went over that edge, D couldn't contain his triumph.

She was wrecked.

"You got chocolate on your pussy." And he laughed.

She threw one arm over her eyes. "Whose fault is that?"

"Pretty sure it's yours." D got a washcloth and cleaned her skin slowly tenderly. Then he wiped the rest of the syrup from his face.

Well, the fucking horse was out of the barn, whatever the hell that meant. So D carried her to his bed and proceeded to worship her body again.

"Oh my God." She collapsed on top of him.

"Jesus, we have got to stop doing this," he panted as his orgasm battered his body, leaving him in an altered stated of consciousness. "We both got reasons."

"It was an accident," she said desperately. "We just… accidentally fell into bed."

"That working for you?" He wrapped his arms around her and rolled, nuzzling her neck and pressing kisses along the curve of her shoulder. Her skin was so soft.

"Okay, no. But we can't undo it."

"But we have to stop."

"I know." She looked as miserable as he felt.

"Last time." Because they really shouldn't do this. He had iron willpower. But for some reason, she got to him the way no one else ever had.

Turns out, Elise on cheat day was his weakness.

Chapter Fifteen

❦

Today was the quarterly meeting of the Billionaire Breakfast Club.

He'd texted everyone last night and they'd all agreed to an interview with Elise. So she was meeting him here after they'd had their breakfast.

With the occasional exception, they all attended the meetings. They would switch up coasts since Pete split his time between Boston and San Francisco, and Duke was in Berkeley most of the year.

D got to the diner first. But within five minutes, the guys were all there.

Peter Nguyen was their resident nerd. These days he worked out and that skinny, socially awkward kid D had met ten years ago was gone. Pete had been the first to hit billionaire status and was his best friend of all the BBC members.

So odd that the geek and the jock were best friends. At first, D had hated Pete. Hated everything about him. They'd had a lot of preconceived notions about each other and they'd both had their share of problems with high school.

But the kid who barely passed and the kid with a perfect SAT score had eventually bonded over the curse of high school stereotypes. D had helped Pete learned to develop his body, and Pete had helped D with his brain.

They clasped hands and did a little chest bump. "Good to see you, man."

"You too." Pete made the motion to push up his glasses that weren't there. He'd had Lasik a few years ago but he still couldn't break the habit.

Jay strode in, and D wondered if he could pump him for information about Elise after the meeting. Although what difference did it make? he thought glumly. He was nothing if not a pragmatist and they had no future.

Duke Kalani, surfer dude and social activist, still looked like he spent his nights sleeping on the beach and his days surfing. His mixed heritage was apparent in his blond, on-the-edge-of-stringy hair and his tanned Hawaiian skin.

The last guy to arrive was Diego Ramos.

"Nice of you to make it." D'Andre mock-jabbed at him.

"I was in the Berkshires," Diego said mildly. The guy looked as relaxed as D.

D was trying to hold onto that sated happy from last night. Because even though it was a mistake, it had been amazing and mind blowing and he wouldn't take it back. But it would seem out of character not to rib Diego.

Jay lifted a blond brow. "Someone got laid."

Shit, Jay could tell?

"Hey, Diego, that's great." Pete's face broke into a huge smile and he saved D from revealing that he'd thought Jay was talking to him. "Me too."

"Jesus, Nguyen. TMI." Duke shook his head.

"Didn't you have your high school reunion last night?" D'Andre asked.

Pete had been looking forward to going back as a successful businessman, to reconnect with his nerdy best friend from high school, and to show the cool kids he'd made it, especially one particular cheerleader. D had been worried about the cheerleader. She'd been a bitch in high school. Maybe she'd turned her attitude around but who knew. He didn't want Pete to get hurt.

"Yes." Pete flushed.

D'Andre high-fived Pete. But wisely kept quiet about his own laid status.

Tracy, princess of high society and Jay's childhood friend, and Courtney, their resident gamer girl—another unlikely friendship—burst into the diner, arm in arm.

Courtney's hardware was prominently displayed, and she was totally gothed out.

Jay frowned at her. "Is that appropriate interview attire?"

Courtney stuck out her pierced tongue at him and shot back, "Is that a silver spoon up your butt?"

D sighed. What the hell was up with Jay and Courtney?

Weirdly, their little band of misfits had become just what Pete had predicted all those years ago. After they'd escaped from the Young Entrepreneurs symposium, they'd traded ideas and talked for hours. Everyone in the odd group had shared what they wanted to accomplish and what they thought they needed to do to get there.

Just like in *The Breakfast Club* movie, they had formed a strange connection.

Except their pact had not only survived, but thrived. They'd been there for each other's successes and their failures, continuing to encourage each other through both the good and the bad.

The BBC had ended up being his sounding board.

They consulted each other. It helped that none of their businesses overlapped. And they'd never steered him wrong.

"What's wrong?" Tracy asked Diego.

"What do you mean?"

"C'mon. It's corporate retreat weekend, right?" Tracy nudged him.

Diego nodded. "Yes."

"How's it going?"

Diego tilted his head, pursed his mouth. "I reviewed the numbers on Thursday and they look good."

Tracy put her hand on Diego's forearm. "Numbers aren't the only component to a successful merger."

"Does this have anything to do with the woman?" D'Andre prodded, finding another way to jab at Diego. Anything to throw attention off him and onto someone else. After all, all's fair in love and war.

Love?

Like a predator scenting weakness, Tracy narrowed in for the kill. "Woman? What woman?"

"It was her," Diego said reluctantly.

Her? This sounded good.

Tracy jerked back. "The little girl? The one who pretty much started your obsession with success?"

"Obsession." Diego laughed. "That's a little harsh."

Nope. Accurate.

"Let's face it," Pete said. "You've always felt like you had more to prove than the rest of us."

Diego blinked at them as if he couldn't wrap his brain around what they were saying.

"Yeah, man." D'Andre shook his head. D still didn't really care if he hit billionaire status. He liked the perks of money and he loved being able to use his earnings for good things. But he was overall a pretty simple guy. "You took that damn name so literally."

Billionaire Breakfast Club.

"Yeah, we're all going to make it." Courtney tugged on her cartilage ring. "Or some version of it, but—"

"Money isn't everything," Jay interrupted her.

She shot him an annoyed frown.

"Easy for you to say, you've always had it." Now Diego sounded defensive.

Duke said, "Dude, it's mostly just a way to keep score."

"Or do something good with. No one person can use that much money," Pete continued.

Jay said, "So what happened?"

"Let's get back to the personal." Tracy rubbed her hands together like an evil genius about to wreak havoc on the world.

"Tell us more about this chick." Of all of them Courtney was the most protective. For all her tough exterior, she had a marshmallow center.

"Maybe he doesn't want to talk about the personal," Jay said, coming to Diego's rescue.

Except maybe he did want to share. "We, ah…" Diego hesitated.

"Wait. This is like, romantic?" Tracy grabbed his hand and clutched his fingers in hers. "Oh my gosh."

"They had sex. That doesn't necessarily translate to romantic." Jay flattened his palms on the table.

"We all know your views on that," Courtney said flatly.

"So, what next?" Duke leaned back into the booth, his arms crossed.

"I don't know. She's amazing." Diego smiled.

D tuned them out, thinking about the upcoming interview. Maybe he could convince Elise to focus on his friendship with the group instead of just him for the profile in *Yankee Sports*.

"Oh goody." Courtney tapped her fingers on the tabletop, her rings clinking. "Let's strategize."

"What are we strategizing about?"

"About the girl." Courtney grinned, her lip ring catching the light.

"But…she isn't business." Diego sputtered.

"The BBC is past that." Tracy was always the romantic. "This is more important. It's life."

D wanted to laugh at Tracy's proclamation…except his own views seemed to be shifting too.

Diego talked out his issues about his girl and D zoned out again. He had nothing to add. After all, he had his own girl troubles.

Elise rounded the corner and just like the first time, he took a hit to the heart.

"Looks like someone else has been struck by cupid." Tracy curled her arm around his shoulder and squeezed. D blinked, glanced around the table but luckily the only other person who noticed was Pete.

D didn't comment. Instead, he tried to surreptitiously gauge how Elise was feeling.

This morning she wore her work clothes. They were bland and boring and did not reflect her personality at all.

But D knew the body under those boxy suits. He started to get hard when he remembered last night with chocolate syrup drizzled over her pale skin. But it hadn't just been sexy, they'd had fun.

The moment she saw him, a smile wreathed her face. Her blue eyes sparkled and her lips curved in pleasure. As she walked toward him, he was thankful all over again.

Damn, he liked her.

With Elise around, his burdens seemed a little lighter, and the world a little brighter, and Jesus he sounded like some sappy pop song.

Had he ever just had fun in bed without the pressure to perform? He'd always instinctively known woman expected him to be their fantasy fuck.

But not Elise.

The sex had been the perfect balance of give and take. Back and forth. Fun and fucking.

She was perfect.

D shoved to standing and strode over to Elise. "Come meet everyone."

Elise had a camera slung over her shoulder and held her phone and a notebook.

When D introduced Elise, he was strangely nervous. He had friends from all walks of life but the BBC were his touchstone. As his emotions teetered, he realized their opinion meant everything as he introduced them one by one.

"Hey, stranger. How's it going?" Tracy's gaze shifted between D and Elise. Something in her eyes gave him pause.

What was that look?

"Tracy, nice to see you again," Elise said. D's brows rose.

"We ran into each other at the club a few weeks ago." Tracy explained.

"Have a seat."

Elise placed her phone in the middle of the table and smiled. "D has told me how you all met, but I'd love to get your impressions on why you're all still together."

They all laughed.

The conversation was a lot of fun. D stayed in the background watching as she put everyone at ease. Each member went around the table and talked about their current projects, and how close they were to that mythic billionaire status.

Elise drew funny anecdotes out of each of them.

"What strange magic did you employ to get Mr. Taciturn to agree to an interview?" Courtney finally asked.

At that, Elise blushed. "Jay set us up."

"Actually, it was my idea," Tracy said triumphantly. "I knew you two would hit it off."

"You sound like a dating service," Jay grumbled.

Tracy blinked. Blinked again. Then laughed nervously. "Of course not. I meant that I knew that Elise would be a good fit for interviewing D'Andre."

"He's a good fit in more ways than one," Pete muttered.

D shot him a murderous look.

While sleeping with her was not the brightest move on his part, for her, if it somehow got out that they had slept together, it would be terrible for her career, which was the exact opposite of what he'd been trying to do to help her.

But it wouldn't get out.

No one knew except them. And neither of them would tell.

He was an expert at keeping secrets. He certainly wasn't going to blab about this one.

❧

AFTER EVERYONE HAD LEFT the diner, Elise sat at the booth, jotting down notes in her journal. She had an hour's worth of recorded conversations from the Billionaire Breakfast Club. She patted her Nikon. She also had several pictures to accompany the article. According to her employment contract, she could freelance side articles that didn't directly compete with her job responsibilities.

As she sipped her coffee, she made a list of possible publications that might be interested in a human interest piece about a very successful group of friends.

D slid onto the chair next to her and propped his chin on his fist. His biceps popped, distracting her.

"I like your friends."

He grinned, his mouth curling in that crooked smile. "Me too."

"I'm surprised they agreed to the interview."

"We're always there for each other."

"Who are you closest to?"

"Pete. We're the original odd couple. The brain and the—"

He stopped suddenly.

Elise ran her finger along the handle of the sturdy coffee mug. "The…?"

Some ugly speculations reared their head. He never read a menu, he had his assistant dictate contract changes, he had no books in his apartment. Those niggling thoughts just wouldn't go away.

"Nothing." His smile was strained. "We're just opposite. He was this skinny little nerdy guy when we met. We had a mutual distrust of the other. But in the end it all worked out. We complement each other."

She wanted to ask him.

Wanted to put it out there, but she was afraid that if she did, he would get angry.

As a test, she pushed her open notebook nearer to his arm. But he didn't even glance at her notes. Not interested. At all.

"You've been a pretty good sport for someone who doesn't like to give interviews."

"I'm trying to open my horizons." D leaned back, arms

crossed over his chest. "Besides, as Jay is always telling me, I have a better chance of controlling the message if I actually give the content."

"So what's your takeaway message?"

"For your readers?"

"Yes."

"Don't focus on only one thing to the exclusion of all others."

"Like football?"

"Yeah." D shook his head. "For the first part of my life, everything took a backseat to ball. If I hadn't met the BBC and begun to think outside of the sport, I would have been lost when I had to quit."

She thought about all the other people she'd interviewed or spoken with who talked about how hard it was for D to quit, but in all their discussions he'd never seemed to mind. At their first meeting he'd given his standard sound bite answer, but maybe now that he trusted her more, he'd tell her the truth. She really wanted to know how he had felt when he quit.

"Did you have to quit?"

"Yes. But I might not have if I hadn't had other options open to me at that point." D rubbed his head. "If football was my only source of income, I might have kept playing to the detriment of my health. When you're backed into a corner, sometimes the only option is to stay."

His words resonated deep in her gut. She needed to learn from his choices and start being more proactive so she wasn't backed into a corner.

"You quit after concussion number three. We haven't talked much about your concussions."

"I had three bad ones."

Which seemed to indicate that he might have had other smaller ones?

"So you decided it was time to quit."

"Chronic Traumatic Encephalopathy is a tragic response to repeated concussions. I would prefer not to blow my brains out or turn violent. The sport has lost too many players in the last few years."

Elise was silent. She was so glad he'd had another outlet. "So making the choice to quit wasn't difficult. But what was the hardest thing about quitting?"

There was a long pause. "My whole life was about football. Then suddenly…it wasn't."

Elise reached out and put her hand over his. "I'm sorry."

D shrugged. "I'm really lucky. I have a great support system. And thanks to the BBC, I started envisioning a future without pro ball before I even started playing. Attending that seminar saved my life."

Her heart expanded like a balloon filling with too much helium until she thought she would burst. "I'm glad for you."

His strength and determination and sheer guts inspired her. "Are you happy with where you are now?"

"I'm constantly reassessing my options and staying open to new opportunities and new ideas."

That was what she needed to do. "How do you stay open to new possibilities?"

"Make a list of everything you've ever wanted to do, whether you have the skills or the means to make it happen right now. Then prioritize them. Then figure out what you have to do to make those things happen. It's not an overnight process, but one small step at a time."

Elise flipped her notebook shut. "You make it sound easy."

"Nothing worth having is easy. Football taught me that. Every skill takes time and energy and practice, practice, practice to get where you want to be."

"Maybe you should write a motivational book," she teased.

His smile disappeared. "You never know."

His sunny demeanor and easy posture was gone and Elise wondered again if there was more to all those little details she'd noticed.

Elise thought about her suspicions that D'Andre Smith couldn't read. Wouldn't that be the scoop of the century?

Chapter Sixteen

❧

Her father was waiting for her when she got home from the group interview.

"Where have you been?"

"Working."

He scoffed. "At that pissant journalism job?"

His dismissal hurt on a visceral level. "Is that why you cut off my credit card?"

"I'm trying to get you to take responsibility for your obligations." He shoved another list at her. "My assistant has set up three more dates."

"I'm seeing Neil again tomorrow for lunch. We really hit it off." She tried to put their plan into place. "I like him."

"The homo? He's a last resort."

"He's a really nice guy."

"You can't guarantee he'll stay with you after the children are born," her father grumbled. "I'm trying to get you settled before anything happens to me. You'd think you'd be more grateful."

Her stomach roiled. She didn't want to get married. But

right now, her only other option was to dig deeper into her suspicions about D'Andre Smith.

She thought about last night. About how she connected with D. About how much fun they had. About how he made her feel. And about who she wanted to be.

She'd been in a state of arrested development since caring for her terminally ill mother. Drifting along, trying to figure out her life. She'd immersed in the nurturing and care of her mother. She'd loved yesterday, working at the Boys & Girls Club. But she couldn't make a career out of that, could she?

Her boss wanted a blockbuster interview. The truth was that D'Andre Smith was an extraordinary man. She'd loved getting to know him, and getting a view into his personal life. Had he gotten through school without learning to read? She wasn't sure. Even if that was true, it wasn't anyone's business but his.

She didn't want to betray his trust.

Yes, she wanted independence. But not at the expense of her soul.

With a sick heart, Elise reached out her hand. "Give me the list."

❧

"ELISE, THANKS FOR COMING IN EARLY."

Her boss had called her first thing this morning and said he needed to see her right away.

"You're welcome, sir." She clutched her fingers tightly together. He was never very chipper but he appeared downright somber at the moment.

"Some disturbing information has come to light." He frowned at her, clearly waiting.

"I'm sorry, you'll have to be more specific. I have no idea what you're referring to." But her stomach was jumping like she'd eaten bad sushi.

"I have it on good authority that you've compromised your ethics by having sex with D'Andre Smith." His mouth turned down into an exaggerated expression of disgust.

"What?" Elise wanted to throw up. "I don't know where you got that info—"

"Your father called me last night."

Her father. Elise froze. A queer buzzing filled her ears blocking out all other sound. Her boss's mouth was moving, his expression filled with a gleeful sort of anger and she finally zoomed back in on whatever he'd been saying.

"When I said that you should sleep with him before you started your interviews, it was not an endorsement or a directive. You should have known that."

Bullshit. He had not been kidding or joking. He'd been totally serious. Not that she'd had sex with D because of her boss. Their connection was intimate. Private. Theirs.

"So, of course, I'm going to have to let you go."

He was firing her.

Those plans she'd been trying to make to find her passion, to find what would make her happy, were dust now. Every time she turned around the way forward felt more opaque. Like a rat in a maze, she couldn't find her way out.

"I'm sorry you feel this way, sir." *Asshole.* "And I'm sorry you'll be losing out on such a fabulous interview."

"Oh, we're still going to run a story. I'll be using your notes to write the magazine profile."

Elise's heart stalled. She'd have to delete her suspicions about D before she turned over her notes. "I'll just get my notes."

"No need." Her boss's smile turned her stomach. "The

server backs up all the company laptops every night. I've read your notes. We've got a blockbuster article on our hands. Of course, we'll have to verify a few things but I'm planning to run the story with the peg about Smith's illiteracy."

"What?" Elise jumped to her feet. "You can't do that."

"No wonder the guy didn't ever do interviews." Her boss chuckled evilly.

"There is no corroboration. That was merely speculation on my part. You can't possibly—"

"Fucking a source is always a bad idea. While the information is slightly tainted by your indiscretions, since I'm writing the article we can overlook the collection methods."

"You can't do this to him," Elise cried. "D'Andre Smith is a saint. He looks out for the community and his family and his former teammates. Why would you even think about publishing that?"

"It's a scoop," he said. "Clearly you aren't cut out for this business."

After she left her boss's office, she was numb.

Fired.

Even worse, the article.

Elise's heart beat at about a million thumps a second. She had to get to D. She had to tell him what was coming. God, how could this have happened?

Her father had not just betrayed her, he'd also dragged D'Andre into his vendetta to get her married, and that was unacceptable. With a heavy heart, she headed toward D's place of work.

It was the first time she'd been to his office. Once again it wasn't what she expected. The vibe was warm and comfortable, sort of like his home, but a little less minimalist as if his employees needed a bit more decoration.

D's assistant, Jamal, an adorable young guy who clearly had a hero worship thing going on, led her to his office.

A wall of glass looked out over the river. In one corner was a post-modern coffee table and sofa. In another was a treadmill and a hanging heavy punching bag. To the side was a credenza with a stack of white towels on top, and next to that a mini-fridge just like the one in his gym, filled with bottled water and the sports drinks he endorsed.

"Hey, come on in. I only have a few minutes but since you're here, I figure it must be urgent." He wore a headset and was clearly listening to something on his phone. "Give me one more sec."

His assistant asked, "Can I get you anything to drink?"

"No thanks, just privacy."

He nodded and closed the office door.

As Elise waited, D was dictating notes about his business plan, rattling off details regarding sports and market share.

Elise sat in the chair across the large black shiny desk without a paper on it. Her heart thudded so hard she thought she might be sick.

Finally D punched a button on his phone screen. He smiled, a bright happy expression, so different from the first time they met.

"What can I do for you?"

Elise stared at him mutely.

"I've got another meeting in a few minutes so I don't have much time."

She didn't even know how to approach this. "I got fired for having sex with you."

He shoved away from his desk. "I didn't say a word."

"Oh, I know." Elise flicked away his assertion. "It was my father."

"Your *father*?"

"Um, yeah."

"That sucks."

"Yeah, but here's the problem." Elise's throat closed, tightened.

"Elise?"

She couldn't make the damning words come out of her mouth. "You never read anything."

D stiffened.

"I noticed in your condo, no books."

"What's that got to do with getting fired?" His voice was cold.

"And you dictate to your assistant, and he dictates back to you."

"Waitin' to hear why that is germane to your loss of a job."

"My boss confiscated my computer…and my notes."

D jerked to his feet. He was the epitome of suit porn today. The suit was European cut with slim legs and a tan tapered jacket over a crisp white cotton V-neck shirt, topped off with glossy cordovan pointed shoes. He wore a shiny gold watch on his thick wrist. She finally realized that seemed to be his one possession weakness. He'd worn at least three different types of watches since she'd met him.

He began to pace. "What's in the notes?"

"I speculated that you might have gotten through school and college without being able to read." She spewed out the words in one long word vomit.

D stopped. Stood preternaturally still. "And?"

"My boss is going to write the article highlighting that. I wanted to give you a heads-up before he calls to verify," she whispered. "Which I'm sure he'll do." It was too explosive to leave out.

"Did it occur to you to ask me?"

"I wasn't ever going to print it or tell anyone."

"And yet your boss has access to those notes." D shook his head violently. His little twists swung against his face. His eyebrows scrunched down over his normally sweet smiling eyes.

"Apparently," she whispered.

"I knew I should never have agreed to an interview." He stared out the window at the river, fists clenched, back and neck tight with anger.

Then he whirled around. "I trusted you," D snarled. "I had sex with you."

She knew he'd be upset, but was he really pissed at *her*?

Chapter Seventeen

"So your goal was to try to influence me to write a soft article?" Elise laughed bitterly. "I guess my boss was right to fire me. I was compromised."

"Not my damn problem," D struck back.

She flinched. "I'm well aware that I'm a problem but you're right. Lucky for you, I'm not yours."

A peculiar shame rolled through him.

It wasn't her fault that he'd hidden his inability to read. But dammit, now everyone was going to know. His business associates, his friends…his mother. Shit, everything he worked for was going to go up in a big fat ball of fire. "Thanks for fucking me over."

"You really are a bastard."

"Pretty sure that's in my bio, baby."

She whitened again. "I am here to apologize. I didn't write the article, I just wanted you to know that I'm sorry."

A lot of good that did him. Years of hiding the truth from everyone. He'd begun to learn to read and he could, very slowly. He was still far more comfortable with hearing the words. He had trained his brain to process sound and so that's how he operated most of the time.

Rage boiled up inside him, bursting from his gut with a direct line to his mouth. She needed to go. Now. "You need to leave." He couldn't even stand to see her face. She'd destroyed everything.

"I can help—"

"Help? You've done enough help." D's fists bunched. "Get out."

Elise's eyes widened. He was too pissed off to try to placate her. He needed to hit something.

"You can be an inspiration to so many—"

"Leave!" he roared and punched the hanging bag so hard it swung into the wall and left a crater.

Her shoulders slumped and she turned away. "I'm so sorry," she whispered.

The moment she left, D called Peter. "I need your help."

"Anything."

"You still in Boston?" Pete split his time between Boston and San Francisco.

"Yeah," Pete said. He was huffing along, horns and traffic sounded through the line.

"How fast can you get to my office?"

Twenty minutes later, Pete burst into his office wearing skintight running gear, sweat soaking his hair. He hadn't even taken off his sunglasses. "What's wrong?"

D dropped into his chair and put his head in his hands. "It's coming out."

Pete grabbed a towel from the credenza in the corner and wiped off the sweat. He regarded D steadily. Just his innate calm had D's heartrate lowering and his breath slowing. "You know overall I don't think this is a bad thing."

"Shit. What if it ruins my whole life? What will this do to my mother—"

"Your mother loves you." Pete shook his head. "This won't matter."

D knew Pete's relationship with his parents was strained.

"What if sponsors and advertisers and—even worse—venture guys pull their support?"

"And what if it makes you even more of a hero?" Pete shot back. "What if your über role model status shoots into the stratosphere because despite a huge handicap you are extremely successful?"

But D couldn't make himself believe that was the logical outcome.

He'd cultivated an image. And shortly, that image was going to implode.

"How did it happen?"

D laughed bitterly. "I let down my guard."

"Elise Putnam?" Pete said, "Funny, she didn't strike me as a bitch."

D fought the urge to defend Elise. She wasn't a bitch.

He frowned. She really wasn't.

Pete was speaking again. "But then again, my interpersonal radar never has worked quite right."

D knew there was more there, but he was still freaking out.

Pete rubbed the sweat from his face and forehead. "Okay. What have Jay and I always said?"

"Control the message." The article wasn't published yet.

"If you get in front of this, you take away their power. *You* control the message." Pete rubbed his hands together. "Call your PR company and let's get to work."

"No PR company."

"You're going to need a team to handle the fallout after your announcement."

"Fine, but right now, just you."

Pete smiled. "Although the circumstances are rough, in the end this will be a good thing."

"Thank you." Pete was the one who helped him start learning to read. D had confessed a few years ago, wondering if his friend would laugh at him. Instead, he'd stuck with D and taught him in secret. In exchange, D had helped Pete build muscles.

"What are friends for?" Pete waved away his thanks. "Ready to get started?"

Before he did, he had a phone call to make. D pulled out his phone and looked for the picture of him and the kid from the camp event. Before he confessed to the world, he was going to start with one small step.

"Who's that?"

D explained about the young fan and his worry that he wasn't good enough in school.

Pete shook his head. "Are you sure?"

"Yeah." A strange relief flooded through him. He didn't have to hide any more. And a weight that had grown heavier with every year seemed to dissolve into the wind.

"Let's get to it. Then I've got to talk to my mother."

Two hours later, he rang the doorbell at his mother's house.

Of all the outcomes of letting this information out, the only person who mattered at the end of the day was his mother.

He could survive without money and his business and

his lifestyle, but he wasn't sure he could survive disappointing his mother.

"Hey, baby. What you doing here in the middle of the day?" She propped her hands on her hips. "And why you ringing my bell instead of using your key?

"Momma, we have to talk."

"What's wrong?" She pulled him inside. "You mess things up with Elise already?"

Elise. His stomach cramped. "About Elise——"

"D. I like that girl. She's good for you." His momma just steamrolled along. "Saw those darling pictures from the Boys & Girls Club yesterday."

"She——"

"I was thinking I'd have you two over for din——"

"She's a reporter!" he shouted.

His mother's eyes widened, then she blinked real slow. She cocked her head, clearly thinking about his shouted revelation. His momma wasn't one to process, she was more likely to react, then calm down later. But she just stared at him, clearly at a loss for words.

"Huh." She plopped into a floral chair that reminded D of the one in his grandparents' home where he'd grown up. "I need time to think on that."

D lowered to the sofa next to her chair, dropped his elbows to his knees and bent over for a moment. "There's more I need to tell you."

"You know I love you no matter what." His mother shifted to the sofa and patted D's back.

D took a deep breath, straightened up and held his mother's hands. "Until a few years ago, I didn't know how to read."

She laughed. "What are you talking about? You went to

college. You got your own endorsements. Your own business." But her hands started to tremble.

"I had people along the way who hid my disability and made it easy for me to hide it."

"But how did this happen?" Her eyes filled with tears and he heard what she didn't say, *how did I not know?*

"It started in middle school. I couldn't keep up so the teachers found ways to get me books on tape, and I took tests verbally. I did the work, I just…couldn't read."

"All this time…" She gripped his hands tightly.

"I can read now. Slowly. I still prefer to listen rather than read. I process things better that way." D wasn't sure how to continue. Shame that he'd hidden this for so long closed his throat, made him reluctant to say anything else.

"Why you telling me this now?"

"It's about to come out and I wanted to explain to you first."

"Because of Elise?" His momma shook her head vehemently, her tight ringlets shaking with anger. "I can't believe that girl would—"

"No. She guessed and her boss found out. Her former boss." And that rage he'd suppressed earlier when she'd been in his office shifted. Now that he'd calmed down he realized she would never have written an article that revealed his secret.

"I still don't understand why you never told me." His momma leaned against his shoulder.

"I'm sorry. I didn't want to worry you. You already had so much on your plate. And my coaches kept telling me they'd take care of it. Somehow it just snowballed until it was too hard to admit. I didn't want to disappoint you."

"I will always love you, no matter what." She squeezed him to her bosom. "I'm proud of the man you've become."

Unconditional love. He was one lucky son of a bitch. He should have trusted his mother and told her sooner. But now that the burden was lifted, he felt freer than he had in a long time. "Love you, Momma."

"Love you too, my sweet boy."

He squeezed her tight. "You know I'm not a boy no more."

"You'll always be my boy. Nothin' is going to change that."

He thought about Elise, about how her father had sold her out to her boss. She'd had the exact opposite support. Her father's love and affection came with conditions and demands.

D had the example of his mother's love, and the support of his friends, while she was adrift, alone. But he would have supported her. He would have given her everything, including his heart.

But instead, Elise's actions had betrayed him.

Chapter Eighteen

TWO WEEKS LATER, ELISE WANDERED LISTLESSLY AROUND
her bedroom as if she could find her purpose in the antique
furnishings and dated wallpaper. But since that day, nothing
seemed to matter.

D'Andre had come out on top of the situation. He'd put
out a press release that very morning and in true D fashion
he'd managed to turn the whole mess into a positive. He had
that way about him.

The picture of him with the boy from the Boys & Girls
Club event had been splashed on every sports and business
page. "Famous Athlete Confesses Illiteracy to Encourage
Fan to Keep Trying." The press release copy was short,
sweet, and poignant. She'd never been prouder. He'd once
again shown why he was adored by fans and critics.

A knock on the door interrupted her pointless
meandering. "Yes?"

"Miss Elise. You need to eat something."

The depression that had gripped her after her mother
died had returned full force. Even her antidepressants
weren't helping. "Not hungry."

Her stomach had been off the past few days, but she couldn't work up the energy to care.

Franny bustled in and stopped cold. "When was the last time you showered?"

She shrugged and slumped into a wing chair by the fireplace. "No idea."

"Honey, you got to get up and get moving."

What was the point? "I'm fine."

"You are not fine." Franny ripped open the curtains and let the sunshine in. "I called Doctor Joanna. She's gonna be here in a few minutes."

Elise squinted at the bright light. She should probably be angry, but the doctor would come, tell her she was depressed, and leave. "I'm sure I've just got a bug or something."

"You got a broken heart is what you got."

Her heart couldn't be broken. They'd literally spent one week together. One. No one falls that fast.

But every day that achy hollow place in her chest was growing like a giant sinkhole. One day she'd just be swallowed up and cease to exist.

About twenty minutes later, the family's personal doctor knocked on her door. The doctor stopped in the doorway when she saw Elise huddled in the chair.

"It's a good thing Franny called me." She came in with her laptop and her doctor's kit. "What's wrong?"

Nothing the doctor could fix.

But Elise dutifully recited her symptoms—extremely tired, lethargic, nauseous. "I'm just depressed."

She'd gotten relatively close to the doctor when she'd come every week to check in on her mother.

Doctor Joanna frowned. "I thought you were getting better."

"I was. But then there was this guy."

The doctor blinked. Cocked her head. Blinked again.

"And our ending was rather spectacular." Elise tried to laugh. "But it's over."

"How long ago did you have sex?"

Two long weeks ago.

"It was only two nights. And we used condoms, plus I'm still taking the pill."

"I want to check one thing." The doctor reached into her bag and pulled out a cup. She seemed…hesitant. "Give me a urine sample, please."

A few minutes later, Elise and the doctor stared at the pink plus sign.

"I guess you forgot when I told you that sometimes antidepressants mess with the efficacy of birth control."

Elise reached out, then curled her fingers, tucking her fists underneath her armpits. "Does that mean…?"

"You're pregnant."

Her first thought was a burst of joy so big she felt like she broke into a million little pieces. A baby? Someone who loved her. Just for her. Who wouldn't give up on her when she made a mistake or she didn't bow to its wishes. Unconditional love.

The doctor was babbling on about blood tests and ultrasounds and other things but Elise just stared at that little pink plus. "I'll do a blood test to confirm but in the meantime, here's a prescription for prenatal vitamins and recommendations for an obstetrician." The doctor patted her hand. "I'll give you a call when the results are in. It should take about a day." And then she left.

Elise placed her palm over her belly in wonder. A baby.

She wasn't ready for a baby. And yet she realized she wouldn't ever complain. This baby was a gift. One she was going to have to share with D'Andre. Facing him again was going to be…difficult.

But she had to tell him.

And then it hit her.

She was working on a new generation of Putnams. Just not what her father had intended when he'd pushed her toward marriage and grandchildren.

Her father was going to freak.

⁂

Elise entered the house.

Unfortunately the positive effects of her long walk to and from the pharmacy were immediately counteracted by the oppressive atmosphere of her family home.

She'd picked up prenatal vitamins and some healthy snacks.

Overnight, she had a reason to get out of bed in the morning. Someone to live for. Someone who needed her. That happy feeling bubbled through her like champagne.

No champagne for her for a few months. A smile burst over her face.

"You need to leave." With one angry sentence, her father destroyed her newfound peace.

She still hadn't told him. She had to tell D first. Elise frowned at her father. "I can just go up to my room if you're entertaining." Usually he wanted her presence to run interference with the kitchen and staff but she'd be happy not to be around any unusual smells. Her morning sickness seemed to get better as the day wore on but she was still learning her way around trigger smells.

"You need to leave this house. For good."

"That seems a little extreme."

"I know what's going on," he snarled. "You're pregnant."

Um, how did he know that?

"The doctor's office emailed a bill with the charge for the pregnancy test. How could you do this to me?"

That was hardly rational. "I didn't do anything to you. Why don't we sit down and talk about this." Her stomach had started to pitch and roll, as if she'd been caught in a squall.

"Unless that baby is Alex or Neil's we have nothing to discuss."

"I thought you wanted grandchildren," she taunted. "New Putnams to carry on the family genes."

"I had specific candidates in place." His face had gotten redder. "Did you do this on purpose?"

"Of course not."

"Your disobedience is beyond extreme." He paced the foyer. Stopped. "You could have an abortion. We could have it done discreetly."

Elise pressed her hands to her nearly concave belly. "I'm keeping this baby."

"Then you aren't staying here."

"You would kick me out when I'm pregnant?"

"Yes!" he hissed. "You've brought shame on our house. Thank God your mother isn't alive to see this day."

"You seriously went there?"

"We did everything for you and this is how you repay us? By shaming the family name."

His words stabbed at her. Elise said quietly, "I spent the past two and half years of my life taking care of Mother. I didn't do anything but find a kind, loving, decent man who showed me an extraordinary passion. This baby has nothing to do with you or your expectations."

"Well then, where is that paragon of virtue now? He got what he wanted from you and he's on to greener pastures."

But he hadn't gotten what he wanted from Elise.

"I don't ever want to hear a word against the father of my child. He's more of a man than you'll ever be."

"Get. Out."

ELISE WAS STUNNED.

Her father had actually thrown her out of her childhood home.

He'd given her time to pack a suitcase and that was it. She'd wasted half the suitcase packing the dress and shoes she'd worn to the fundraiser the night she went home with D. Elise stood on the sidewalk beyond the brick-and-iron gate. The sun was still high in the early evening sky. But the place she called home seemed foreign and hostile now.

She headed toward Boston University and the T in a daze, rolling her little overnight bag behind her. The heat of the day was still trapped in the cement sidewalk and shimmered over her face.

She'd only gone about half a block when an older Honda stopped next to her. "Go 'head and get in." Franny gestured to Elise while looking over her shoulder.

Elise shook her head. "I'd hate for you to get in trouble because of me."

"Best kind of trouble." Franny frowned. "Where you going?"

"I…don't know."

"Well, I have an idea. But I don't know if you'll like it."

Elise said, "I started planning a few weeks ago. So I have a little money. You can take me to a hotel."

Neil. She could call Neil.

He'd called several times to check on her after the D debacle. His boyfriend had dumped him and they'd commiserated, sort of. He'd even talked about her coming to work for him but they hadn't made any firm plans.

Franny said stubbornly, "First do this one thing."

Elise didn't want to upset Franny so she agreed. They drove for about five minutes, only a few blocks over, and pulled into the driveway of another house in Brookline.

"Who lives here?"

"Come on and see." Franny practically dragged her out of the car.

Elise did not have a good feeling about this, but she texted a quick note to Neil and asked if they could meet for coffee, or decaf tea in her case, tomorrow morning.

He agreed.

Franny rang the doorbell.

Within moments Mary Smith, dressed in a shimmering dress of gold and silver, opened the door.

"Franny. What were you thinking?" Elise cried. "I'm sure I'm the last person Mrs. Smith wants to see." *She probably hates me.*

"Come on in," Mary Smith said not sounding like she hated Elise at all.

Elise shuddered. "I'm so sorry. I don't know why she brought me here."

"'Cause I told her to."

That shut her up.

Mary Smith led her into a warm farmhouse-type kitchen with white cabinets and stainless-steel appliances and glass-fronted cabinets.

"A reporter?" Mary shook her head. "He done fell for a reporter."

Fell for? He hated her.

Elise said, "You have to know that I never intended for anything bad to get out."

"I read your article."

D had already outted himself in very public fashion, so Dick Johnson and *Yankee Sports* had changed the tone, focusing on D's accomplishments in spite of the fact that he hadn't been able to read. Her boss had published the article she'd mocked up almost word for word as she'd written it.

"You admire my D'Andre."

"Of course I do," Elise said softly. "He's an amazing man. You raised him well."

"You like him?"

She more than liked him.

"According to Franny, your heart is broke."

Probably. But she'd get over it. She'd have to. And she was going to want Mary Smith in her life. She had no intention of keeping her baby from him or her grandmother. And she didn't want any more lies between them. "Yes."

Mary preened. "You still coming to my party?"

Elise had forgotten. "It's tonight?" That's why she was all dressed up.

Mary Smith nodded.

"You don't really want me to intrude on your big day."

"I want you there."

But what about D? "D won't want me there," she said miserably. "And I don't want to cause a scene."

"My son knows what's good for him," Mary said stubbornly. "He won't cause a scene."

Chapter Nineteen

❧

D GHOSTED AROUND THE OMNI BALLROOM, DOUBLE-checking the last minute details. He wanted the night to be perfect for his momma.

Everything was ready to go. All they needed was the guest of honor.

She obviously wasn't surprised about the party. And he wanted her to be happy, but his heart wasn't in it. His mind was on the last time he'd been in the hotel. He'd met Elise at Parker's Restaurant downstairs and been knocked sideways. That feeling had yet to go away.

Momma had invited Elise to this party. His heart pinged. He wanted her here. Hell, he just plain wanted her.

And he missed her.

But he'd be shocked if she came.

He'd tried to get in touch with her, but her phone was either off or she'd blocked his calls, because the messages showed as undeliverable. She didn't want to talk to him.

He couldn't really blame her.

He'd been brutal the last time he'd seen her. Once he'd calmed down and analyzed what had happened, he'd known that he'd hurt her. Elise would have never exposed him that way. She should have asked him instead of speculating about his ability to read. But if he were honest, he probably wouldn't have told her the truth.

And that made him acknowledge that the mess had been as much his fault as hers.

But he hadn't been able to apologize because she wasn't taking his calls.

Once this party was finally over, he was going to tell her how he felt.

Since attire was semiformal, he was wearing his tux again. Rare for him to get this dressed up twice in one month. The black suit just reminded him of Elise and how much he'd messed up.

The guests started pouring in to the ornate ballroom. The crowd was going to be eclectic. Ballers from his pro days, because his momma had been a fixture on the circuit. She hadn't missed a game. Some of the football players' parents. His momma's church group. And the Billionaire Breakfast Club, who'd all met his mother when they'd come to watch him play pro ball.

Diego and his new girlfriend, Penny, were first to arrive, with Duke right behind them. They were staying at the hotel for the night. Penny started talking to Duke, and Diego made his way over to D.

"Where's your mother?" Diego glanced around the ballroom.

She should be here soon. "Sent a limo."

"Way to do it up in style." Diego smiled, then turned serious. "How's it going?"

"Been better." D shrugged. He couldn't pretend to be happy but at least for tonight he needed to let go of the moroseness.

"You still haven't been able to get in touch with her?"

Needing advice, D had talked to Diego about the situation with Elise. Diego was the only one of the BBC who was attached. "No." And just like that he wondered if he should stop. Clearly she didn't want to talk to him.

They'd been together for one week. One. Not even one week.

Diego glanced across the room at Penny. "Regrets, man. Wouldn't you rather regret trying with her than always wondering?"

Penny glanced up from her conversation with Duke, and her smile lit her whole face.

D was curious. "You gave up a lucrative business deal when you chose Penny."

"I gained everything when I told London to shove it." Diego's grin said it all. "You know what you've got to do."

"I do."

Diego clapped him on the back.

"The second I see her again, I'm going to talk to her."

"Well, that might happen sooner than you'd think." Diego's eyes were wide. "Did not see that coming."

"What?" D imagined the worst. Someone in a fight.

Diego poked him. "Check it out."

D turned, his stomach clenched, prepared for a disaster —instead he was struck dumb.

Elise walked in next to his mother, looking pale and unsure, but his momma had a firm hand curled around Elise's biceps.

What the hell was happening?

He headed toward the pair, but his mother broke away from Elise and kept moving. D had to wish his momma happy birthday first so he followed quickly, afraid Elise would disappear before he could talk to her.

He finally got through the throng wishing his momma a happy birthday. He scooped her up in a giant hug. "Happy Birthday."

"Thank you, sweet boy."

"What did you do?" The words burst out of him. How, why, so many questions.

"Don't sass me." She shooed him. "Go talk to that girl."

D wanted to but he needed his mother to understand. "She's a reporter."

"She's a woman first. And you been miserable without her."

"This is important, real. I want her."

"Well, don't you think you should be telling her instead of me?"

"I just don't want to hurt you."

"Seeing you hurt is what hurts me." His mother's voice softened. "I want you to be happy, D."

"She makes me happy."

"I already figured that out." Mary Smith's smile was wise, gentle. "Now go tell her that."

His momma didn't raise no dummy. "Yes, ma'am."

But when he turned around, on the other side of the room, most of the BBC had surrounded Elise.

Oh, this could be bad.

⁂

ELISE DIDN'T KNOW what she was doing here.

Somehow Mary Smith had steamrolled over all her objections and here she was at the Omni, dressed up for her birthday party.

D was not going to be happy to see her, but somehow

Elise had been unable to deny her unborn baby's grandmother.

So she had hovered in the doorway of the ballroom, her gaze flitting through the crowd of people, searching for his broad shoulders and crooked smile.

Her heart yearned to see him. But she was afraid that once he saw her, his rage and disgust would come roaring back. She wasn't sure she could handle that today.

She finally saw him chatting with Diego Ramos.

He looked…good. Great.

A group of people came up behind her and Elise shifted to the edge of the entrance, trying to stay unobtrusive. But suddenly she was surrounded.

"What are you doing here?" Pete Nguyen came up on her right.

"Oh, um, I'll just get out—"

"No." That came from Tracy Thayer. She gripped Elise's arm tightly. "Not until you explain."

Her stomach curdled, and she had to hope that her body wouldn't take this moment to betray her.

The BBC crowded around her.

"This is a surprise." Jay raised his blond eyebrows.

"I know." Elise's stomach churned. So far they weren't completely eviscerating her, but she wondered if it was coming. "I'm sorry." Of course she was going to have to talk to him one on one at some point, but tonight was not the time to spring on him that he was going to be a daddy.

Pete shook his head. "We're not the ones you need to apologize to."

"Will you tell him I'm sorry?" Because they were the gauntlet. They were the people who would have D's back.

Courtney, Jay and Tracy stood in front of her, blocking

her way into the ballroom, where she didn't want to go anyway. Standing like a wall between Elise and D.

"I didn't mean to hurt him," she blurted out.

"I would hope not." Courtney shoved in front of Jay.

The BBC was his family, his support, and they would take good care of him. No matter what. She had to get out of here. She couldn't do this tonight. "You guys…take care of him."

Her gaze shot to where she'd last seen him, but D was gone.

"Why can't you take care of him?" Jay narrowed his gaze, skimming over her.

She would love to. But D didn't want her. Not a word in the past two weeks. Not a word. But she wasn't about to reveal her private torment to these people. "His mother—"

"His mother loves him." Pete snapped, "Try again."

Mary Smith *had* brought Elise to her party. And maybe they weren't trying to get rid of her because they weren't telling her to leave.

"But I hurt him," she said desperately, wanting them to yell at her, to defend D. Because she knew they would protect each other to the death.

"So why are you here?" Courtney frowned at her.

She whispered the truth, "Because I couldn't stay away."

"Have you ever felt this way about anyone?" Tracy asked quietly.

No. She shook her head.

Pete, who knew D the best, pressed her. "Then what are you going to do?"

Elise didn't have a plan. She thought about how much she missed D. You couldn't fall that fast, could you? "I don't know."

"Well you better figure it out. Fast." Pete said, "And so we're clear, if you hurt him again, I know people."

Elise almost laughed at the threat.

"I'm not kidding."

Elise put her hand on Pete's arm. "I'm glad he has you."

And she knew what she had to do.

Elise whirled, ready to go find D. And ran straight into the wall of his chest.

Chapter Twenty

D LOOKED FORBIDDING.

His trademark smile and easygoing demeanor were nowhere to be found.

The food she'd forced down earlier threatened to come back up. All the scents and smells in the ballroom were dancing in her stomach, and definitely not with joy. She would have to talk to him another time. "I'm sorry. Your mother insisted I come. I won't stay——" She knew how special this party was to him and she didn't want to do anything to mess it up. They could talk later.

"I have something to say." He was somber, his jaw tight.

No welcome in sight. She placed her fingers on his wrist. "Can we do this someplace more private?"

"Are you sure you don't want to stay here?" Tracy said avidly.

She didn't want to cause a scene at his mother's party. "Private would be best."

"I have no problem talking in front of my friends."

Of course he didn't. "You're very lucky to have them."

D squinted for a moment, then nodded. "I booked a suite for my mother. We won't be interrupted up there."

"Okay." She took a deep breath. "Let's go."

The BBC melted away as they left the ballroom.

They rode the elevator in silence.

Once they were in the room, D began, "I need—"

"I need—"

They both spoke at once.

Stopped.

They both spoke at the same time again. "I'm sorry."

"I'm sorry."

Elise paused. Swallowed. "I'm the one who needs to apologize."

"We need to put it behind us. And move on." D cupped her shoulders and bent his head to kiss her.

His lips touched hers, and he felt like coming home, like everything she'd ever wanted in one perfect moment.

When she didn't pull away, D deepened the kiss. Slow, gentle, with an underlying tenderness that nearly broke her heart all over again.

She'd missed him. It seemed impossible. They hadn't known each other long and yet they'd just clicked. But he still needed to know everything.

Elise broke away from him. "How are you doing?" she asked. "Since the article came out."

"Good. I'm good." They were stilted, awkward. "So far the response has been mostly positive. 'Cept for a few unhappy people but haters gonna hate."

"And most people love you." She smiled but it was bittersweet. "You have to know that I never meant for anyone to see those notes."

"I know." He shook his head. "After I calmed down, I

realized that you wouldn't have done that to me on purpose."

"Of course not. You're entitled to your privacy."

He knew her intentions were not bad, but that was a long way from forgiveness.

"So how are you doing with…" she waved her hand "…the fallout."

"I'm really good." He smiled but made no move touch her again. "The biggest surprise was the support of the venture capitalist money guys."

"That's…great." His fame quotient had actually gotten a huge bump up when the news came out. Not that she'd been happy because she'd been the catalyst. But at least it hadn't impacted him negatively. She didn't know what she would have done if his career had taken a hit.

"Yeah. It's been nice not to worry anymore about my secret getting out. The shift in my stress level has been amazing."

"I'm glad it all turned out okay for you. No thanks to me…or my father."

"So we're good?"

She could only wish. Elise was wringing her hands. She thought she'd have more time. She thought she would duck out early and call him later, tomorrow, next week, next month. But she was here and they were in the same room and he was talking to her. At least for now. "I have something to tell you."

"We can talk later." He bent his head again. And she almost let him take control and forget about her confession.

"I can't get sidetracked." She pushed him away gently. "I need to—"

"I need you." He wrapped his arms around her and tugged her into his embrace.

All she wanted was to snuggle in and absorb his touch, but she had to get this out. "I'm pregnant," she blurted out.

D froze.

Pure shock widened his eyes.

"Not on purpose, of course. I would never do that to you." When he didn't say anything she started babbling. "Turns out antidepressants can affect the effectiveness of birth control and remember when the condom leaked a little—"

"Stop." He barked in a gruff voice.

She stopped and took a deep, deep breath. Her heart sank. She smoothed her fingers over his broad chest and down the lapels of his tux, not looking at him. "I know we'll have a lot to figure out with logistics and visitation, but I'd like to save that for later."

"A baby—" he said faintly. "Later…meaning you want to keep the baby." His words were measured, slow, and lacking in any kind of emotion.

She had no idea what he was feeling. Clearly he wasn't overjoyed like she had been when she first found out.

"Of course I'm keeping the baby. But I would never try to trap you. Right now my primary concerns are eating right and figuring out where I'm going to live."

And then the room was full of silence.

He made no move to touch her again. Hope had swelled inside her, opening a giant black hole, but all that yearning crumbled, smashing into the abyss when he remained quiet. At least he wasn't angry with her.

Elise kissed his cheek, paused for just a moment to inhale his scent, take it into her heart and capture it there so she could bring it out when she was lonely and longing for him.

Then she stepped away from him. "You're a good man, D'Andre Smith."

It was time to go. She'd said everything she'd needed to say to him. She'd apologized. She'd told him about the baby. She pressed a hand to her belly.

Her baby was going to have a kick-ass father.

He tilted his head. "If you think that, then why didn't you return my calls?"

"What calls?"

There was a bite to his words. "I've called pretty much every day since you left my office."

She shook her head. "I…didn't have any missed calls from you." She pulled out her cell phone—at least her father hadn't cancelled her service yet—and scrolled through her contacts.

She pulled him up.

"See, no calls from you."

"Because you blocked my number."

"No. I didn't." But she peered at the screen and he showed as blocked by her provider. "My father must have done this." He must have requested that D's number be blocked. "You have to believe me, I didn't block you."

She grabbed his hands, held his fists in her palms. He had called her.

"So you weren't blowing me off?"

"No."

"And you think I'm a good man? Worthy?"

"Of course. Our baby is lucky. I couldn't ask for a better man to be the father of my child."

D tugged her against him. "So why did that sound like goodbye."

"Of course it wasn't goodbye. We'll have to see each other as we co-parent."

D MADE A FACE.

Co-parent. Jesus, he hated the sound of that word. But maybe she wasn't interested in pursuing anything, in exploring their connection.

A baby.

They were having a baby together. He was one part thrilled, one part terrified. And when he'd considered trying to get her back he hadn't really thought beyond them being together.

"Not gonna lie, this throws a wrench in my carefully constructed plans," D said.

"I know." Elise flushed.

She didn't know anything.

"Actually I have no plans. I just knew I needed to get you back." That was the most important piece of this whole night. He wanted her back. As long as they were together, they could deal with anything.

"I should be more sorry." She placed her palm over her flat belly. "But ever since I found out, I realized that I want this baby."

"You know my background. I would never walk away from my child."

"I know that," she said softly.

She did. Because she knew him.

A baby. They were having a baby. He didn't know anything about being a father. But then he realized he knew plenty about being a good parent. His mother had been the best. And Elise would be amazing.

But when he'd been considering what to say to convince her to give him a second chance, he hadn't been thinking about anything but step one.

"My only plan was to get you back in my life." He'd been miserable without her. "I thought we could…date. See where this leads. I didn't want to walk away without trying."

Her smile lit the entire suite. "I'd…like that."

"Clearly things are a little different now." He reviewed the past few minutes. And suddenly he backtracked. "What do you mean, where you're going to live?"

"My father kicked me out." She laughed bitterly. "I have some money for a hotel for tonight but I've got to make more permanent arrangements."

Her father? That bastard. "Seriously? Come live with me."

"We shouldn't go from dating to living together in one conversation."

"Why not?" He wanted to shout from the rooftops.

"D. We barely know each other, and for the sake of the baby we owe it to our child to go slowly. To get to know each other and keep our relationship positive for him or her."

"I can be positive."

"So can I. But let's face it, you're a serial dater and I've only had two relationships before you. We shouldn't rush into anything."

"Seems to me we've got a timeline." D lifted her into his arms, gently. "Nine months and counting."

"I'm still not living with you. At least not right away." Elise curled her arms around his neck. "I need to learn to live on my own before I even consider moving in with you."

He thought about her life up to this point. "Okay. But let's agree to revisit the subject before the baby is born."

"Agreed."

D carried her toward the bedroom. "But you need to know that I really like you."

"I really like you too." She tucked her head into the curve of his neck.

Hope flooded him. He looked around. "Hey, we're in the Harvey Parker suite."

Elise studied the elegant living room area. "It's nice."

"The day I met you, I wished we could end up in this suite."

"Really?" she said drily.

"Yeah. I felt like I'd been hit by a D lineman. Dizzy and dazed and dazzled by you."

"Oh." She melted against him.

"And then you opened your mouth, and you knocked me sideways again."

"I remember feeling the same."

"Seems a shame not to start working on dating right now."

"Right now?" She laughed breathlessly.

"No time like the present."

And they were a little late to the party.

Epilogue

THREE MONTHS LATER

Elise used her key to let herself in to D's condo. She'd just come from work and was planning on spending the night. They spent more nights together than they did apart. But she'd still learned to survive on her own two feet.

She'd ended up getting a job with Neil's public relations firm. She had a real knack for the social media arena. She was renting a room in Mary Smith's Brookline mansion. There was a little bit of a conflict of interest because Mary made no secret of the fact that she wanted D and Elise together.

Mary was thrilled about the baby and had become a surrogate mother to Elise. Her father had yet to speak to her. She had managed to contest the terms of her trust and now had a small stipend in addition to her salary. And while some days she was sad that they no longer had a relationship, the rest of her life had flourished with her independence.

D had been bugging her to move in with him and she was thinking it might be time.

"I'm home!" She tossed her house key onto the little stand next to the door. And went in search of her baby daddy.

Elise placed her hand on her belly. She'd felt the baby kick today!

Just a flutter. And at first she thought maybe her morning sickness was coming back. But then her heart had literally wanted to explode as she realized that the baby was saying hello. She couldn't wait to tell D.

"Where are you?" she called. "I have something I need to show you." And tell him. She was ready. They were ready for the next step. She hadn't ever really thought you could fall in an instant, and she was still happy that they'd taken it slow, but it was time.

Elise walked into the kitchen. A bowl with lemons sat on the black granite island and dishtowels with a graphic of the Tobin bridge hung over the handle of the oven. Little touches had turned his place into theirs.

"I have something to show you too." His wicked grin promised that she'd like it.

❧

D WAS WAITING in the kitchen for his girl.

She came in smiling and glowing with health and vitality. His heart nearly hurt looking at her. He was so grateful that their friends set them up.

Before he could say anything, she squealed. "The bookstore."

The bag was over on the end of the counter. "Uh, yeah. I stopped in while I was running errands."

They were both working crazy hours, and Elise got tired

quickly. So they spent plenty of nights cuddled in bed reading…after he rocked her world, of course.

"This is what you wanted to show me." She dug through the bag, completely ignoring D. She clutched the latest release from one of her favorite romance authors to her chest and her eyes shone with glee. "You remembered."

He tapped his head. "I remember everything about you."

"What else?" She pulled out the other books.

A middle grade mystery, that one was for him, and a chunky laminated book of *The Very Hungry Caterpillar*.

"You got the baby their first book."

"Can't start too early."

A shimmer glistened in her blue gaze. "Oh, D," she said softly.

And he shifted uncomfortably.

"Oh!" Her smile lit up his formerly cold kitchen. "I got sidetracked."

"What?"

She grabbed his hands and placed them on her belly. "Put your hands here."

"What are we doing? 'Cause I can think of more interesting places to put my hands," he teased.

But then he felt it, the barest of taps against his palms. "Is that…?"

"Yes." She nodded, her face full of wonder, and he knew this was the perfect time. He hadn't been kidding when he'd said he had something to show her. It just wasn't what she thought.

D's heart beat like he'd just run the fastest forty of his life. "Lightning round?"

She laughed, just like he hoped she would. "Sure. I think

my stomach can handle it. What are you thinking? Pickles or ice cream? Sweet or tart?"

D dropped to one knee.

Her smile disappeared. "What…"

"Only one question. Yes…or no?" He flipped open the blue Tiffany box and held it out to her.

Her hands rested on his shoulders lightly, and pure love filled her warm blue eyes with tears. "Yes."

D slipped the understated ring, a simple two carat diamond cut in the shape of a heart, on her finger. The past three months had only cemented the feelings that had knocked him loopy at their first meeting. "I love you."

"Get up." She tugged at his sweatshirt.

"In a sec." Shit he probably should have gotten more dressed up for this, but he'd picked up the ring this morning and he'd known he didn't want to wait one more day. "You and the baby are everything I wanted." Even if he hadn't known it at first.

D spread his palms over the slight bulge that was growing by the day. "I love you too, little one." He closed his eyes and pressed his lips to the mound.

"D," she said faintly. "Get up."

He rose to his feet.

She cupped his face, kinda like he'd touched her belly and stared into his eyes. "I love you too."

She kissed him with her eyes and heart wide open.

"I can't wait to see what the future brings, what our baby brings."

She put her hands over his, the three of them joined together. "It will be everything we never knew we wanted."

PENNY AND DIEGO: A second chance at happiness won't come easy when their reversal in fortunes and unexpected sexual attraction complicates everything. Will they be able to work through their regrets and memories, and learn that love is the greatest fortune of all? Find out in His Semi-Charmed Life (Billionaire Breakfast Club #1).

Thank you D and Elise's story! I hope you enjoyed reading Everything He Wants as much as I enjoyed writing it. If you did enjoy this novel, below are a few ways you can help a writer out!!

GOOD: Lend the book to a friend

BETTER: Recommend the book to your friends

BEST: Leave a review at Amazon, BN, iBooks, Kobo, Google Play, Goodreads...basically any place they sell or review eBooks. Every review helps my work get out to other readers and I cannot even express how much it means to me when you let people know you liked my work. Readers have so many choices nowadays and limited dollars to spend. It can be difficult to take a chance on a new author even if the premise sounds appealing. By reviewing books, you give other readers insight into the story world and help them make informed purchases.

THANK YOU, thank you, thank you for your support!!

. . .

P.S. Would you like to know when my next book is available? You can sign up for my new release email list/newsletter at <u>Lisa's Confidants</u> I send out newsletters once a month typically filled with info on upcoming books, friend freebies, and contests I'm involved in. I will never sell or distribute your email to other people.

Want to see how Diego and Penny got to their Happy Ever After? Read on for an excerpt of His Semi-Charmed Life ....

Excerpt of His Semi-Charmed Life

June 1997

Worst. Summer. Ever.

Diego Ramos strode out to the parking lot, ignoring the rules to go check on his precious car. His '69 Charger had gotten him here but he'd lost his muffler on the way up. He'd growled the final miles to Camp Firefly Falls on the faulty part.

He'd been working on this car forever. He was finally old enough—sort of—to drive it, even though he'd been tooling around Dot illegally for the past few years.

He was working all summer to pay for the muffler at cost. He'd been planning to buy the one Tío Raul had at his garage. But before Diego could scrape together the money, one of Raul's full-paying customers needed one and his uncle couldn't turn down the sale. Their family friend Hector said he might be able to get his hands on a replacement. Might. But if he got a full paying customer, Hector had to sell it to them, because he needed the money too.

It was the worst to be stuck here. He totally understood

that if they had buyers while he was here at camp, he was screwed. He had to stay at camp to make enough money to buy the part.

He kicked at a stone, sent it scuttling into the brush that lined the path.

A single spotlight on a post cast more shadows than illumination over the lot—which was really just a decent-sized opening between two stands of trees.

Diego opened the hood. Not a squeak. He took damn good care of his baby.

He stroked the sleek, clean engine like he was petting his little cousin's cat. "Soon, baby. You'll be all prettied up," he crooned to the engine like she was a girl.

He flushed, glanced around, but no one had seen him talking to his car like she was real.

Diego climbed up on the trunk of his car and lay back to stare up at the stars. The Charger was the one constant in his life. His mother and father were in and out. He had bounced from relative to relative until his uncle got married a few years ago and then he'd gone to live with his tío and tía permanently.

His uncle got him this camp job through one of his customers. Diego was supposed to be thankful for it. He was. Sort of. He'd never tell anyone but he missed his little cousins, Raul Jr. and Zinnia, even though they annoyed him ninety-nine percent of the time.

One thing he'd give to these mountains, the sky was amazing. Light from the stars twinkled in deep blue mysterious space.

"What'cha doing?"

He jerked up so fast his head went dizzy.

And there she was.

He *hated* working here. Little Miss Princess Penelope

embodied every single reason. She was only like nine years old and so damn smug. She'd been whining since her parents dropped her off at the beginning of the week. They were in Europe. Without her. *Boo. Fricking Hoo.*

"You're not supposed to be out here," he snarled. Dammit. Why was she here?

Penelope Hastings stood there looking at him with those stupidly innocent, bright green eyes. "Neither are you."

"Get back to your cabin." Except he was going to have to take her. He couldn't let her wander around in the dark. Part of his job was making sure the campers were safe.

"Why are you so upset?" She stepped closer to his car.

Her pout caused everything to bubble up inside him. Couldn't he get frustrated and angry in peace? Couldn't he have one damn minute alone? Apparently not, if he wanted enough money to keep fixing up his baby.

"Let me take you back to your cabin." Diego sighed. He slid off the trunk, dropped to the dirt and gravel parking lot, then took a second to stroke his palm over the blue paint before he gently eased the hood closed.

She danced back a step. "Is something wrong with your car?"

"Yeah."

She frowned, her ginger eyebrows crinkled as if the concept of car problems was beyond her. "Why even bother working on that old piece of junk?"

Junk? Maybe to her it was junk but to him this car was everything. It was freedom. It was life. It was his future.

"Aren't you only fifteen?"

And she was nine. They'd done the whole introduce yourself in a circle on the first day. So he knew her name was Penelope Hastings, she was rich as fuck, and so super sad that her parents had left her at camp instead of taking her to Europe.

"So?" So he'd driven here slightly illegally. So the fuck what? He had his permit.

"Well, if you're only fifteen—" She laughed, a delighted trill of sound, like the birds in the forest only softer, and weirdly sweeter. "When's your birthday?"

He trudged toward the line of cabins where the girls stayed. "September."

What that had to do with anything he had no fucking idea. Of course, he never claimed to understand rich kids. They lived in their own stupid bubble.

She clapped her soft pale hands and laughed again. "Well then, silly. You only have to wait a couple more months and you'll get your new car for your sixteenth birthday!"

She dropped the words so eagerly, so happily, as if she'd magically solved his problem and everyone in the fucking world got a car when they turned sixteen.

"That's about as likely as the Red Sox winning the World Series."

"I don't understand."

"Welcome to the real world where kids don't get new cars on their birthdays, you spoiled brat." Shit, he was going to get in trouble for that. He was a counselor. And he needed this job so he could afford the parts for his beloved car.

Yeah, the owners made it seem like they were all equal and happy and shit, but the reality was, Diego worked for Miss Richy-Rich Hastings.

"Oh." Her face fell, her brows scrunched together as if she were actually trying to imagine a world where kids didn't get a new car when they turned sixteen. "So not everyone gets a car?"

Could this kid be any dumber?

"There's a whole world of people who don't have food to eat at night, don't wear shoes without holes." Ugh, she glanced down at his feet and his ratty old Converse. "And don't get new cars. So, no."

"That's…too bad."

"Yeah, it's a real fucking nightmare."

Her shoulders slumped. Her dark ginger hair was almost Charger Red in the soft light of the parking lot.

"Well," she said brightly, her smile reappearing. "My dad always says, 'How do we turn this failure into a success?'"

"I'm a failure? Thanks for making your opinion loud and clear."

God, he hated her. She was everything he wasn't. Clean and perfect. Her blindingly bright white tennis shoes and her naïve, always smiling face versus his threadbare high tops, soles so worn they were just about to crack, and his scowl.

Her smile faltered. "Oh no, of course not. He just says, 'When things don't go the way you planned, you work with what you've got, and turn that negative into a positive.'"

"I've got *nothing*." Diego spit out the words. He wanted, with an agonizing pain in his heart, to throw some dirt on her. To ruin that sparkly perfection so she was as dirty and grumpy and mean as he felt inside. "So get the hell out of here, you stupid little rich girl."

Tears filled her bright green eyes. She lifted her trembling chin and shot him a vengeful glare. "I was just trying to be a good friend."

"Yeah, well, I don't need any friends. Go away."

She finally ran down the path toward the cabins. He should go after her, follow her and make sure she got back to her cabin without harm. But he flung himself on the hood of the car.

He was so getting fired.

As he lay there, his initial rage simmered and stewed as he kept reviewing their conversation. And dammit, the picture she painted wouldn't leave him.

A new car for his sixteenth birthday. The promise that he'd never go cold or hungry again. The shiny idea that he could turn a failure into a success dangled out of reach like a sparkling lure on the hook of life.

He lay under the stars dreaming of that life and ignoring the reality that he was probably going to get fired. Which would mean no new part for his car, no awesome life, no perfect future.

But in the morning, a subdued, less sparkly Penelope Hastings never said a word to the camp director. She also never spoke to Diego again. He knew he should apologize. But he didn't.

That regret festered in his heart. Once he got back to Dorchester, he decided he could apologize next summer. But after that first summer, he'd been able to work in his uncle's garage, learning more about cars and mechanic skills. Then camp closed and he never got the chance to apologize.

But he never forgot her.

Twenty years later

It was so fucking dark up here.

The night sky was liberally sprinkled with stars but that light didn't lend much visibility here on the ground. In the woods there were no street lights, no street signs. He was tired, cranky, and if Zinnia, his pain in the ass assistant and cousin, was here right now, he'd personally cut her salary.

Diego creatively cursed his cousin, his late departure, and the world in general.

He didn't want to be here.

His 2007 Porsche Carrera GT really didn't want to be here. At the rate he was bumping over the uneven ground, his suspension was going to need a realignment tomorrow.

The camp held nothing but bad memories. Except…his recall of the little girl who'd had a profound impact on the course of his life was complicated. Regret and gratitude all rolled together.

Some days he wondered if he would be where he was if it wasn't for little Penelope Hastings and her blind optimism. Which was why he hadn't blasted Zinnia after she booked this retreat.

Finally, Diego arrived in the clearing. The deserted clearing.

There were only two cars in the matted down grass and gravel parking lot. Then he remembered—this was the employee parking lot. There was probably a separate one for guests.

Diego pulled up next to a sweet, perfectly restored Charger. He got out of the silver metallic Porsche, ignored the empty camp and instead bent to peer at the leftover remnant of his youth. The car was an exact replica of his very first car. The one he'd lovingly restored. The impetus for one of the worst moments of his life.

The paint job was perfect, the Bright Blue Poly an original color. She also had a white racing stripe with a hint of metallic sparkle in the paint.

God, he'd loved that damn car.

In the distance the faint sound of music drifted on the

still summer evening. Fireflies buzzed in the thin woods. He spied the path to the main lodge.

He tried to dredge the camp check-in details from his brain. But he'd mostly tuned Zinnia out when she'd been admonishing him not to be late.

He was late.

It wasn't exactly his fault. He'd gotten caught up in contract negotiations with his company's lawyer, and Jeffrey London, the CEO of London Automotive. They were in talks to merge London Automotive with Ramos's Classic Auto Restoration. Diego was on the brink of the culmination of twenty years of planning and ambition.

To Diego's delight, the Billionaire Breakfast Club was about to indoctrinate another member.

And he couldn't wait.

Merging was a solid business decision. Ramos's Classic Auto Restoration had gotten big. They were all working extra hard. If they merged, the company would be bigger but there'd be more people for work distribution. London's business dovetailed well with Diego's. Their combined company would seriously increase his net worth.

But as Diego cast one last longing look at that Charger, he realized he hadn't geeked out and wrenched on a car in…he couldn't even remember.

He sighed.

Tinkering with a classic car wouldn't increase his bottom line, and a gearhead wouldn't get bigger and better in a coverall with grease under his fingernails.

He grabbed the leather suitcase from the passenger seat and headed toward the registration tent through the trees. A circular driveway was empty. The canvas structure in the middle of a grassy expanse inside the circle held a 6 x 2 foldup table and a plastic green file box closed tight. A single

Papermate pen rested in the crevice between the file box and the table surface.

That was it.

He pulled out his cell phone so he could call Zin.

No service.

Diego sighed. The main lodge was down the path not too far in the distance. He'd check in there.

The single porch light cast a warm yellow glow over the painted wooden balustrade. As he walked toward the light, he searched the shadows and realized the camp seemed awfully empty and quiet.

The ground was slightly squishy. It must have rained up here sometime this week. He grimaced when he thought about the mud clinging to his Italian loafers and dampening the bottom of his silk trousers.

Diego strode up to the lodge. Muted laughter and music came through the open window. He rang the doorbell.

"Coming!"

Within in seconds, the door flew open and a woman tumbled out.

Rich auburn hair framed her sun-kissed classic bone structure. She had tanned cheeks with a smattering of freckles across her nose, a lush full mouth, and remarkable bright green eyes, the exact shade of classic Charger Rallye Green. She sparkled with amusement and happiness and an inner glow. She held a tumbler of white wine in long elegant fingers with short unpainted nails.

"Oh, hello." She straightened her plump lips, trying to contain the laughter that had graced her features when she'd opened the door.

Diego frowned. She looked…familiar. Except not. He had an excellent facility for remembering faces. That skill had served him well in business. He ran her features through his memory banks. She was there, just out of reach. As if he *should* know her.

Except for that single light, the porch was bathed in darkness.

"Ah, can I help you?" She fiddled with the tail of a man's plaid shirt over her camisole. The thin white cotton revealed small breasts with an intriguing shadow in the valley between them. Her faded loose jeans with holes in the knees were rolled up to reveal delicate ankles and toenails painted a surprising bright neon green.

Like a wolf, his body was instinctively attuned to her. Her features tripped some switch inside him, primitive and needy. His brain stuttered on those bright toes, thinking about how he'd like to start at the arch of her foot and spend hours discovering the secret hollows and erogenous places on her body, just like he learned each nook and cranny and idiosyncrasy of a 5.7-liter HEMI V-8.

"I'm here for the camp," he blurted out when he realized he'd been quiet for far too long.

"Okay." In the background, Third Eye Blind's 90s hit "Semi-Charmed Life" played. The furniture in the living area had been pushed back against the walls. A coffee table was littered with two empty plates and a mostly empty bottle of wine.

"Penny. Did I hear the doorbell?" Another woman, brown curly hair and generous curves, skidded into the room. "Can we help you?"

"I'm here for the camp," he said again clearly, but he finally clued in to the fact that no one else was here. Just these two women.

Diego was still in his suit and tie, the offending silk noose now strangling him.

The woman who answered the door blinked. "The one

that starts tomorrow?" Now she was hastily trying to shove her hair into the knot at the top of her head.

"Tomorrow," he said flatly.

Diego pulled his phone from his pocket. His lifeline. Everything was on the state of the art smartphone. He accessed his calendar. No. "According to my calendar, it was supposed to start today."

"I'm sorry——"

"Dammit." He was going to kill Zinnia.

The redhead straightened, the smile disappearing from her face. "Excuse me?"

"Not you." Diego had figured out what happened. Zin made sure he was here before camp started by giving him the wrong date. "My assistant."

He punched the button on the phone and returned it to his pocket.

"She entered the date incorrectly?"

He twisted his wrist, stared at the roman numerals on his watch, and blinked at the time. It was after ten at night. No wonder they hadn't been expecting him.

"More like an end run," he muttered. "What time tomorrow?"

"Two," the curvy brunette said.

Diego sighed. He was tired. He'd started his day at five a.m. and had been running ever since. He rubbed his hand over the stubble on his jaw and sighed. "I'll be back."

"You can't leave now." The redhead propped one foot on top of the other and leaned against the door frame. "Briarsted doesn't have any hotels. There's no place to stay nearby. Right, Meg?"

Diego certainly wasn't sleeping in his car. Those days were long over. He propped his fists on his hips, and his stomach growled. Loudly.

The grinding in his stomach that was near constant these days ramped up its slow attack on his body. Stress and hunger were not a good combo.

"There's got to be an empty room in the lodge," Penny, the auburn-haired goddess, said to the other woman. "Right?"

"Let me just turn off the music."

"Clearly, I've interrupted your…evening," Diego said politely. "I'll let you go."

At the same time, Penny said, "We were just dancing."

His gaze skimmed between the two very attractive women. "I'll let you get back to it."

"Oh! No, we're not." Penny laughed, a light trill of sound, as her eyes twinkled with a mirth. Something about that laugh triggered another flare of lust deep in his belly. "It's fine. You're fine."

"He certainly is," Meg said under her breath, but Diego heard her.

Okay. Not lovers then.

Lover. The word conjured hot nights, liquid sighs, fevered kisses…and oddly the woman who'd answered the door.

He didn't have time for a lover. But damn if his mind didn't zoom right back to the redhead when he realized the two women were only friends.

"Come on in and we'll figure out a place for you to sleep." The brunette shoved out her hand. "I'm Meg, the camp chef, and this is Penny. She's going to be running a corporate farm team-building experiment."

Diego tried to keep the grimace from his face but he must have failed because the chef laughed.

"It will be fun," Penny said defensively. "I promise."

Her gaze skimmed his silk suit, pressed shirt, and Italian

tie. "Although hopefully you've got something more casual in that bag. Farming, and camping, are messy."

Her smile was wide, and her white straight teeth bit into her unpainted lip.

Meg said, "I can't check you in, no idea how that works. Let me show you a room where you can crash, Mr.....?"

He was more addled than he thought. Combo of a long day and the intriguing Penny with the neon toenails and the mysterious green eyes.

"Diego Ramos." He held out his hand so he could shake hers.

He couldn't help but notice Penny's reaction. She'd jolted, her bright green eyes wide.

Did he know her?

Acknowledgments

It's been a crazy year. I moved from California (packed up twenty years of life and put it in storage for four months) to Massachusetts (lived in a hotel, then a rental house before moving into our new house).

Needless to say, life has been a wild ride lately. This book is a long time in coming but I'm so glad D and Elise are finally here. I had a lot of fun writing their story.

Thanks to Tawdra Kandle and the rest of the #MeetCute authors for inviting me to be part of such a fun concept.

Huge thanks to my editor, Deb Nemeth, for being so patient with me after I pushed out my deadline multiple times. Thanks to Meg Murray for the awesome cover.

And big squishy thanks to Vanessa Kier and Adrienne Bell for FaceTiming with me so I didn't have complete withdrawal from my Bay Area writer peeps.

<u>Family Stone Box Set (Stone Cold Heart, Carved in Stone, Heart of Stone, Still the One, & Jar of Hearts)</u>

<u>The Nostradamus Prophecies</u>

<u>View To A Kill #1</u>

Never Say Never #2

<u>ALIAS</u>

Stalked (ALIAS #1)

Hunted (ALIAS #2)

Vanished (ALIAS #3)

Saved (ALIAS #3.5)

Deceived (ALIAS #4)

<u>Billionaire Breakfast Club</u>

His Semi-Charmed Life (Billionaire Breakfast Club #1)

Everything He Wants (Billionaire Breakfast Club #2)

She Feels Like Home (Billionaire Breakfast Club #3)

Coming July 2021 Sideways (Tracy's story!)

His Road To Paradise

His Dirty Little Secret

About Lisa

USA Today Bestselling Author Lisa Hughey started writing romance in the fourth grade. That particular story involved a prince and an engagement. Now, she writes about strong heroines who are perfectly capable of rescuing themselves and the heroes who love both their strength and their vulnerability. She pens romances of all types—suspense, paranormal, and contemporary—but at their heart, all her books celebrate the power of love.

She lives in Cape Ann Massachusetts with her fabulously supportive husband and one somewhat grumpy cat.

Beach walks, hiking, and traveling are her favorite ways to pass the time when she isn't plotting new ways to get her characters to fall in love.

Lisa loves to hear from readers and has tons of places you can connect with her. It's a wonder she gets any writing done at all….

Be Lisa's Friend on Facebook
Sign Up for Lisa's Confidants
Visit Lisa on the Web

Follow Lisa on Pinterest
Follow Lisa on Instagram
Email Lisa
Be Lisa's Friend on Goodreads
Like Lisa on Facebook at Lisa Hughey Author